The Devil's Rider

Trilogy

by
Joanna Blake

Printed in the United States of America
First Printing, 2014

Pincushion Press
http://pincushionpress.tumblr.com/

Wanted By The Devil

By

Joanna Blake

Chapters

1

Someone was following her. Again.

It was a perfect day. A warm, early summer day in the middle of June. The sun was shining, the birds were singing.

Kaylie picked up her pace and hurried down the hill toward North Avenue. She had just picked up her diploma and was carrying it home, along with the contents of her locker. Graduation had been a week ago but she'd had to skip it, just like she skipped a lot of things. Sometimes it seemed like all she did was work. School work, homework, house work, work work. She'd been out the last few weeks of high school due to mono but her grades had carried her through. She was an excellent student thank God so her teachers had been lenient.

Mono. What a joke.

They called mono the kissing disease. Like anyone ever kissed her.

It wasn't like she was unattractive. Kaylie knew she was cute. Hot even. With long light brown hair and big brown eyes, and tawny golden skin she knew she had a pretty face. The kind you see in magazines even, with pouty lips and high round cheek bones. Her body was curvy too, despite walking literally everywhere due to a lack of wheels. Her large breasts had made her feel embarrassed when she'd first got them a few years ago. Big and perfectly circular over her absurdly tiny waist and long legs. Her body made her look older in a way that belied her innocence. But she was innocent. Painfully so.

Halfway through her junior year, all the boys in school had abruptly left her alone. They didn't just stop flirting with her or trying to get her to go out with them, they started avoiding her gaze, even pretending that she didn't exist.

It was weird.

Even Janet had said something. Before the sudden change it had been

Kaylie who got all the attention from boys. Suddenly it was just the opposite, with her loud mouthed best friend having a date every weekend, not her. Janet was realllllly helpful, just saying that they must have found out about her cooties. Still, they'd both caught the shift, so Kaylie knew she wasn't imagining it.

That was around the same time she'd started noticing the bikes. Wherever she went, whatever time of day, it seemed like there was always a bike behind her. Not just a bike. A *bike.*

It wasn't so crazy to see hogs around. She did live in California. And her town was the epicenter of one of the biggest clubs in the state. But still. It was weird.

She glanced over her shoulder and saw a huge old school motorcycle driving slowlllly up the street behind her. He wasn't looking at her. In fact, he was looking everywhere but at her.

Who knew bikes could even go that slow? And why would he if he wasn't following her.

It was definitely weird.

It had all started when she was serving the counter at Mae's, the diner that everyone still called the soda shop. It had been there since the 1950's, more or less unchanged. She'd worked there since the age of 14 when her mother had insisted she get a job if she wanted to go to college someday. It was out of their reach otherwise, but she'd promised Kaylie would be able to go, no matter what. *If* she worked hard, at school and elsewhere.

Kaylie had taken her mother's advice to heart, and her mother had been true to her word, helping Kaylie save her money for school and making sure the bare necessities were met at home. But it's not like she could afford to buy all the cute outfits that some of the girls at school wore. She had learned to stick to the basics and buy one or two things a year that could go with anything. One pair of jeans, one skirt, one plain blouse, one sweater. That was it. Her wardrobe was not extensive or trendy but it worked as long as she limited the colors she bought. Pink, navy, white, denim. She didn't look frumpy but sometimes she longed to just go to the mall and pick out whatever she wanted. Someday...

It hadn't stopped guys from asking her out in droves though, not until Junior year anyway. She'd just started dating when she could, in between shifts at Maes and working extra hard to make the honor roll. True, she hadn't had a lot of time, but there had been plenty of offers. An absurd amount really. She'd gone out with a few of the boys at school but never let any of them get past first base though. And now, nada.

It's not like she wanted to get pawed in the backseat of a camaro. But it was hard wondering what was wrong with her. Why she was the only girl in

school who'd never had a boyfriend...
or a prom date. Not that she could have
gone to the prom with mono!

She sighed. What was even the
point anymore? It's not like any of those
high school boys compared to *him.*

Devlin McRae.

It had taken some doing, but she'd
found out the name of the guy who'd
started coming in almost every time she
worked a shift. The guy with the tousled
blond hair and green eyes. The guy who
looked rough, like he had a past, but who
was always polite and left her absurdly
large tips.

Everyone seemed to know who he
was except her. They all gave him a
respectful distance when he came into
the diner and sat invariably at the
counter, near the end where the
waitresses took their breaks between
tables.

That was how she ended up
spending so much time in his vicinity. Not
talking, just... nearby. She tried to ignore

the feelings that he created in her, the nervous, jittery tingles, but it didn't really work. She looked forward to seeing him, dreading it at the same time. She was a great waitress when he wasn't in the diner. When else did she drop coffee cups?

She'd decided that if she was going to have a crush, she'd better find out who he was. He rode a bike, she knew that much. He was a little older than her too, in his early or mid twenties. He had a hard look to him but that wavy blond hair was incredibly boyish. Not to mention all those muscles...

No one had wanted to talk about him at first. The name had been hard enough, but finding out that he was the President of the local MC had taken even longer. At 25, he was the youngest President in the history of the club. Devlin was a bad boy for all intents and purposes. Most likely a criminal and definitely the leader of a bunch of criminals and soon to be criminals. Off limits to someone like her certainly.

But dear lord, he was dreamy. As if a model was dressing as a biker for a high fashion photo shoot. He was the real deal though. Dangerous. She could look at him though, right? There was no harm in that... She was subtle about it, just sneaking a peek now and then. That's until she realized *he* was watching *her.*

She'd dropped another coffee cup when she'd caught his eyes on her for the first time. Her whole body had lit up like a christmas tree. He hadn't looked away either. Just sat there, watching her clean up the mess on the floor. When she stood up a few minutes later, he was gone.

And a twenty dollar tip was on the counter.

That was around the time she started noticing the bikes. It never felt threatening. It always felt more like they were escorting her. They didn't stare or cat call. The huge guy with long curly hair nodded at her now and then. That was it. They were just... there.

She turned around and saw the same curly haired guy who was often behind her. He reminded her of a bear, or a villain from an action movie. The guy looked *intense*. As soon as she turned the corner to her block though, he was gone. As usual. Well, not gone, but waiting politely around the corner in case she went out again. Kaylie lived on a cul de sac so it's not like she could get past him. Not unless someone hid her in the trunk of their car.

She almost laughed. The whole situation was bizarre. It's not like she could call the cops or them. 'Um, yeah officer? There's this guy-well it's not *always* the same guy- but anyway it seems like there's always a biker half a block behind me. No, they don't actually *do* anything...'

Yeah, that would go over great.

She wasn't sure she even wanted to call the cops anyway. Not if the crazy thought she'd been having lately was... true. The crazy thought she hadn't even admitted to herself or the two girlfriends who had noticed the bikes. Janet and Lindsey had been freaked out by it at first but now they didn't even mention it. Just part of the scenery to them. But Kaylie couldn't stop thinking about the possibility.

The crazy idea that just felt like it just might be true.

She was starting to believe that they were keeping an eye on her. Protecting her. For Devlin. It was a crazy thought because he'd given her no real reason to believe he even knew who she was. He'd never asked her out or said anything remotely flirtatious to her. He just placed his order and sat there quietly, eating his food, always utterly relaxed and confident. He could have owned the place the way he sat there. He could have owned the world.

But the way he looked at her whenever he came into Mae's... she caught him watching her hungrily constantly now. He'd stopped hiding his purpose in being in the diner all together. Eventually she'd learned not to flinch or drop anything from the incredible heat coming off the man. He was smoldering. For her.

That much she knew was not her imagination.

Kaylie ran to her house and got dressed for work. She had a shift tonight and as usual, they needed the money. She was attending state school starting in the fall. She could commute from here but ideally she'd be able to get an apartment on her own. Never mind books and bus fare back and forth every day. It was over an hour to campus by public trans. She was not looking forward to that.

Besides, once school started she wouldn't be able to work as many shifts. She'd miss it. Mostly because of Mae of course. But if she was honest with herself she'd also miss bumping into *him*.

I wonder if they'll follow me onto campus?

She giggled at the thought of bikers parked outside her lecture hall and slipped into her pink rayon uniform. Mae's was old school. She didn't mind though. The retro waitress uniform did look pretty cute on her.

2

She poured another cup of coffee for the trucker at the end of the counter. It was already past the end of her shift, nearly 11 o'clock. The whole place would be shut down already if they didn't have one last customer. Charlie, the line cook, was already shut down for the night and only waiting for her out of courtesy. The staff were all very protective of her, especially since she'd started working the late shift.

Kaylie sighed and rested her face in the palm of her hand. It had been an uneventful evening. No sign of *him* tonight. Mae and Sally the afternoon waitress had both left a few hours ago leaving Kaylie with no one to talk to. She'd restocked the entire diner and even read a few chapters of the new book she'd borrowed from the library. But now she was starting to long for bed.

She thought about drinking some coffee herself but she knew she'd be up half the night if she did. She nursed the chocolate milkshake she'd made for herself earlier instead. Everything was already wiped down. She wanted to go home.

Finally the trucker got up and left, putting a few bucks on the counter. Kaylie put the money into the register, pocketed the tip (35 cents) and ran a rag over the spot where the coffee cup had been. Charlie had already put the cup and saucer in the dishwasher so they were out of there in two minutes flat.

She waved goodbye to Charlie and stepped onto the sidewalk, pulling her old wooly cardigan closed in the front to keep warm. It might be June, but it still got cold at night sometimes. It was eerily quiet too, making her look around for her usual motorcycle escort. They were nowhere to be seen at the moment.

She sighed and stepped out onto the sidewalk, turning the corner off the main road.

"Need a ride?"

Kaylie stopped dead in her tracks. Leaning against his bike was a very handsome, very clean shaven, very wrapped in leather and tight jeans Devlin McRae.

Her heart stopped. She stood there dumbfounded before she remembered to take a breath. Inhale. Exhale. In and out. In and out...

Had he been waiting for her?

"Hi."

He grinned and looked up at her from under that lock of blond hair that always seemed to be falling just so over one eye. Her stomach dropped nervously at the come hither look in his green eyes.

Bedroom eyes. So that's what that meant.

He had definitely been waiting for her.

"Hi."

She swallowed nervously, wishing she had drank a cup of coffee after all. Maybe she'd be quick witted instead of standing there like a dullard when the most beautiful, and by far the most dangerous man she'd ever laid eyes on was - what? Asking her out?

No. Not out. He was offering her a ride. That was it. No big deal, right?

It felt like a very big deal. Too big a deal for her to say anything clever certainly.

He didn't seem put off by her silence though. He just held out his hand. There was a helmet in his other hand. For her.

"Don't worry, I'll go slow."

She could have sworn there was something sensual in his smirk as she saw herself putting her hand into his. He wasn't just talking about the bike. He was talking about... other things. She stared up at him as he slid the helmet over her head, locking the chin strap into place. He ran his thumb over her cheek as she blinked up at him, completely under his spell.

Snap out of it girl!

Before she knew it she was behind him, her legs straddling the bike, with her skirt pushed up her thighs. Her arms wrapped tentatively around his taught midriff. Even through the worn leather jacket she could feel his muscles. He had a lot of muscles.

"Hold on."

She tightened her grip as he revved the motor and took off. Her cheek was pressed against his shoulder, and suddenly she could smell him. He smelled like oil, leather and something else she couldn't quite put her finger on. But overall he smelled masculine. Very, very masculine. The rumbling of the bike underneath her felt odd, making her all tingly inside.

Had she been cold before? Because suddenly she was burning up.

****

They rode around the outskirts of town before he headed back toward her house, clearly taking the long way. He pulled over a few blocks from home and turned the bike off. He turned his head and glanced at her over his shoulder.

"Do you need to go right home?"

She shook her head 'no.' Even though she knew her mother would worry if she took too long. Even though she had no idea what Devlin wanted, or anything about him really.

That wasn't exactly true though was it? She did know. She knew he wanted her and she knew he was protective. And tough. But he was always sweet to her. That's all that mattered, right?

Besides, nothing on God's green earth would keep her from going with him tonight. He could have taken her to the moon and she wouldn't have said a peep. The little voice in the back of her head reminded her this was beyond foolish but she ignored it. She knew instinctively that he wouldn't hurt her. Not physically anyway. Protecting her heart was another matter altogether.

He picked up speed as he turned up the mountain road. Recognition set it, along with a renewed feeling of nervousness. He was taking her to the overlook. He must be. That was the only thing up there.

Lovers lane.

Her heart was thudding in her chest as they climbed the sharp curves that led to the infamous make out spot. He took the steep road with ease and confidence. She felt completely safe on the back of his bike. What she was worried about was what would happen when they stopped...

Would he kiss her? Would he want more? It was obvious he liked her. At this point there was no point in lying to herself about that. She liked him too. No, she *wanted* him. She had for a long time.

Now that she had him though, she had no idea what to do with him.

They pulled into the clearing and suddenly the kickstand was down and he was helping her off the bike. There was a knowing look in his eyes when he took off her helmet. He could probably see her blushing! But no- it was dark here. The thought gave her a small measure of comfort. He took her hand and led her over to the rocks overlooking the valley. You could see two counties from up here.

Kaylie watched nervously as he walked unerringly toward a large flat rock and guided her onto it. He sat beside her and stared out at the view. She decided to do the same thing and caught her breath in wonder.

"It's beautiful…"

He looked at her with a hint of surprise.

"You've never been up here before?"

She shook her head shyly.

"No. I mean, not at night."

That made him grin for some reason. Oh. Of course. He could probably tell how ignorant she was about… well everything. She felt ridiculous sitting beside the sexiest man in town like a nun. She realized she was sitting on her hands and yanked them up and into her lap.

He put his arm around her and pulled her against his side. And then... nothing. He just sat there. He was wearing fingerless gloves that scratched her skin when he started to stroke her arm. Her sweater had slid off her shoulder and he was- oh!

Tingles shot through her body from the place where his fingertips brushed her, making lazy circles. With a shock she realized her nipples were getting hard. There was a warm feeling was growing between her legs.

The sensation was unfamiliar to her, strange and exciting. But she knew instinctively what it was. It was desire.

He pulled her in for a kiss, somehow sensing the exact moment that the tides had tipped in his favor. The urge to be close to him was finally overwhelming her nerves. Her lips parted slightly under the pressure of his. He had surprisingly soft lips for a man. Not that she'd ever kissed a man before. A boy, yes. But this was a different matter entirely.

****

Devlin inhaled the scent of the innocent young beauty in his arms. She tasted so sweet, fresh and clean and... chocolatey.

"Hmmmm... you taste good."

He lifted his head to look at her. Her eyes were still closed and a dreamy expression was on her face. He liked it even better than the blush she'd worn when they first arrived. She didn't know it, but he had excellent night vision.

He lowered his head again, before she could come to her senses and wonder why a nice girl like her was kissing the head of the most notorious Motorcycle Club in the county. Hell, the SOS were feared statewide. He grinned and slid his tongue along the soft pink lips, urging her to open her mouth. When she finally did, he eased his tongue inside, twirling it against hers. She let out a startled gasp before settling down again and letting him work his magic on her.

It was clear she hadn't been kissed much. He grinned into her mouth. Instead of turning him off it inflamed him more than he could have imagined. He liked her innocence. He liked it *a lot.*

Of course, he was the one who made it clear to all the young men in town that she was off limits. That was nearly two years ago, and clearly whatever experience she'd had at that point was halted in it's tracks. Once he'd put his claim on her, no one had dared to approach her. He suspected they had barely looked at her in all that time. Safer that way. Better than looking, and wanting... he was the one who'd had to watch her grow up and blossom into the beauty in his arms. He was the one who had been forced to wait.

He pulled her closer, resting his hands firmly on her hips. He resisted the urge to squeeze her round bottom or slide his hand up to her breasts. If she was any of the other women he'd bedded over the years, they'd be undressed and underneath him already. But he'd waited this long for Kaylie, and he could wait a bit longer.

Not *too* much longer though. The bulge in his pants was already becoming uncomfortable. Better to stop for now. They had time. If he had his way about it, she'd be available to him every night from here on out.

Forever.

He gritted his teeth and lifted his head. He'd stopped sleeping with the girls who hung around the club a few weeks ago, knowing that it was almost time to make his move with her. She was the sort of woman that you didn't mind giving up cheap thrills for. Besides, he had a feeling there were plenty of thrills ahead. For both of them.

"I better take you home now. Don't want to worry mama."

****

She nodded, ashamed to admit to herself that she didn't want to leave. Didn't want him to stop kissing her, touching her, maybe even more. She'd forgotten completely about the time. She glanced at her watch and gasped. He was right. Her mom *was* going to be worried. Normally she'd be home by now. No, an hour ago. Dang.

He helped her onto the bike, fixing the helmet into place again. Then he swung on gracefully and kicked the throttle. She wondered how many times he'd done that. Thousands probably. He made it look so easy, like a panther leaping into a tree. Every move he made was clean and spare, without any added flourishes. She rested her cheek against the leather of his jacket, inhaling deeply.

Her relief was palpable. He hadn't pushed her to stay out or go further than she wanted to. In fact, if anything, he'd left her wanting more.

They pulled up to her house, making her realize that he knew where she lived. Of course he did. He'd been having her followed, hadn't he? She bit her lip as he lifted her off the bike and undid the strap of her helmet for her. He ran his thumb over her lip this time, his eyes hooded with desire.

She closed her eyes, hoping he would kiss her again.

"Hi Devlin."

Kaylie jumped at her mothers voice but Devlin didn't move. She peeked up at her mother and was surprised to see a placid look on her face as she smiled benignly at the man who'd driven her home on his motorcycle.

"Good evening Mrs. Thomas."

He grinned and winked at Kaylie's shocked expression. He leaned down and placed a soft kiss by her ear.

"You didn't think I was going to take you riding without asking permission did you?"

Her mouth was open as he climbed back on his bike and rode away.

Her mother gestured her inside with a knowing grin.

"What did he-"

"What did he ask me?"

"Yes, and when?"

Her mother grinned and locked the door behind her.

"That's between him and I. Now off to bed. You have a long day tomorrow."

"I do?"

Her mother just smiled and kissed her goodnight.

3

Her mother shook her awake at 8 am. Every fiber of her being longed to stay in bed. She hadn't slept late in so long...

"What is it? Is everything okay?"

"Yes sweetheart. Devlin is picking you up soon."

That got her attention. She sat up.

"He is? What for? *How* soon?"

Her mother shrugged and said "About ten minutes. I'll let him tell you about it. But he said to wear something comfortable and bring a sweater. You'll be out all day."

Kaylie was on her feet in seconds, already in panic mode. Her mother turned back from the hallway before looking over her shoulder coyly.

"Don't forget your bikini."

"WHAT?"

She ran after her laughing mother, swatting her bottom. Why did her mother know more about what her - she didn't know what to call Devlin, not yet anyway - *she* did? She grinned suddenly, realizing he must have arranged all of this yesterday or even earlier. Asking her mother for permission was sweet... and unexpectedly old fashioned for a biker.

She felt warm inside at the thought. And if her mother approved... all the better.

It had been just the two of them for so long, ever since her father had passed away. Having someone else besides Mom looking out for her was nice. She was afraid to think about anything past that. Who knew what his intentions were really? But he was making her wonder if he was after more than just a summer fling. He did seem to be extremely prepared... and determined.

She ran into the bathroom and took the world's fastest shower, giddy with excitement. She slipped into her one bikini and pulled on a pair of cut off jean shorts and a white top with pink flowers covering it. She debated about what to do with her hair and decided to leave it down but to bring a clip so she could pull it back later. It would just get flattened by the helmet anyway. She stuffed a sweater, sunblock and lip gloss into a bag and was chugging a glass of orange juice when she heard the rumble of a bike outside.

He was here.

Devlin rode through the warm June morning toward Kaylie's house. He was pleased, despite everything that had gone down last night. The club was considering taking on new members and had hazed a few promising new prospects from the group that had applied. Things had gotten a little out of hand with one of the young guys and now they had a prospect in the hospital with third degree burns. Dave Fahey had been drinking heavily and dared the foolish kid to shoot flaming liquor out of his mouth. The kid would be alright- he'd even earned the club's respect by not screaming like a woman. But he'd have a pretty big scar and would be forever be known as whisky beard.

Dev hated stuff like that though. It wasn't what the club was about. It was supposed to be a brotherhood of guys with their own code. They had a set of rules and morals that worked, outside and set apart from the rest of society.

The average rule following American was a sheep, but the Spawn were the wolves.

Sure, getting hammered was a right of passage for the guys and a way to blow off steam. But not every night. And hurting each other was wasteful- they had enough enemies in the state who were willing to do it for them- on both sides of the law.

He pushed aside the thought of the local law enforcement- Sheriff Dooley in particular had a hard on for Devlin. His second in command Officer Grant was just as bad. He now got facetious parking tickets on a weekly basis. He often found himself with a tail when he was out on his bike. It had forced him to slow down his breakneck pace considerably. But nothing was going to ruin today. He was going to help Kaylie celebrate her graduation and introduce her to the club and their old ladies. Sure it was fast, but he'd been laying the groundwork for years. He'd made his decision. And it was obvious to him that Kaylie was on board with it.

He grinned, imagining her wearing his jacket- and nothing else. Her hot little body had felt so good pressed against him last night- all warmth and sweet innocence. Well, for now anyway. He didn't bother pretending he'd let her stay innocent for long. He wasn't a man used to denying himself. Definitely not when it came to women.

This wasn't going to be easy.

Then again, nothing worth doing ever was.

He pulled up to her house and parked his bike. Before he could even climb out she was coming out the door looking like sunshine and promises. He felt an odd feeling in the pit of his stomach as she came toward him in a pair of cut off jean shorts and a pretty floral blouse. When she got closer he saw the strap of a bikini top peeking out from around her neck. It was yellow and white gingham.

Damn but she looked fine!

He had the sudden feeling that he might be the one who was out of his depth, not the innocent 18 year old virgin walking toward him. She moved so gracefully, her sweet little body swaying in an unconsciously seductive way. He swallowed, his mouth feeling dry.

She stared up at him trustingly with her big brown eyes while he fitted her helmet over her soft golden brown waves. He couldn't help but brush his hand over the softness of her cheek before helping her onto the bike and climbing on in front of her. He lifted his hand, waving to the woman watching them from the stoop. She waved back with a stoic expression on her face.

It was a good thing he'd been working on Mrs. Thomas for a few years now. He'd made sure the woman hadn't lifted a bag of groceries from the first day he'd noticed Kaylie. She was a smart woman. She knew it wasn't a bad thing to be connected to the club in this town.

She'd never have to deal with a flat tire, or a bothersome neighbor. They'd take care of everything for her.

He grinned to himself as he pulled away from the curb. Kaylie arms snaked around toward his stomach sending a jolt of arousal straight through him. It wasn't a bad exchange at all.

4

He hadn't told her where they were going and she hadn't asked. It only occurred to her how odd that was after they'd been riding for a half an hour. She'd been too absorbed by the sensation of the bike, the scenery, and him. Most of all him.

It didn't really matter anyway. If he wanted to surprise her, she'd let him. Even if she wanted to ask him, it would have to wait until he pulled over. There was no way he would hear her over the rumble of the bike.

It was the sort of thing that should make her hate traveling this way. Clinging to him, with zero control over where they were going, how far or how fast. But she didn't hate it at all.

She loved it.

It surprised her how much she loved it. The speed, the smell, the incredible riskiness of it all. But most of all, she loved that she wasn't riding alone. They were together. Fused into one. She trusted him implicitly. Maybe it was foolish, but it was true.

They'd left town far behind already and were heading through endless fields of corn and other crops. She felt her curiosity rise again. There was nothing out this way, unless he planned on taking her over the state line. What was he up to?

It was another ten minutes or so before she realized where they were going. The lake. The County Fair. Child like excitement flowed through her. If she could have jumped up and down, she would have.

It had been years since she'd been to the County Fair. It was easily an hour away and her mother didn't have the time or money to travel for frivolous reasons. Kaylie had always loved the little day trips they'd taken as a family, when her father was still alive. It had been a yearly event for them. After he passed though, the trips had stopped. A lot of things had stopped.

She didn't blame her mom though. Raising a child alone was difficult, and she didn't have an extended family to help out. They'd had family time in other ways. Mostly the sort that involves hard work and chores. Every Sunday after church they spent a few hours cutting coupons. It was fun. Well, kind of.

Kaylie's mother wasn't the sort to kick up her heels or laugh at something just for the fun of it. That had been Kaylie's dad. The joker, the prankster, the life of the party. She missed him each and every day. Her mom did too. It was obvious what she was thinking about when Kaylie caught her gazing out the window or just staring into space. She did that a lot.

Dad had been the one who came up with the fun things to do. He always had a plan or a game to play. But he could be serious too, like about making sure Kaylie knew that she had self worth. He'd instilled that in her early.

'Don't be a pushover Kaylie. Stand up for yourself.'

She'd listened to him when he said that. She'd heard.

She was still thinking about her father when they pulled up to the camp grounds next to the fair. Devlin parked the bike near a row of Harley Davidsons. A bunch of people waved at him but he just nodded and helped her with her helmet.

"Are you hungry?"

She shook her head.

"Thirsty?"

She shook her head again.

"Do you need to use the facilities?"

"No, thank you."

He grinned as if that were the cutest thing he had ever heard. For some reason, it annoyed her that this big tough man was treating her like a puppy. A desirable puppy, but a pet all the same. She frowned at him.

"What's so funny?"

"So polite. It's adorable."

Her cheeks got warm as he leaned down to kiss her. It was only their second kiss and this time it was in broad daylight. She sighed as his lips pressed into hers. His arms slid around her waist to her lower back. His hands were warm and-

"Dev! I hope you're hungry! We're grilling already man!"

Devlin lifted his head with an exaggerated sigh. Kaylie giggled at the look on his face. He threw his arm over her shoulder and walked toward the group of bikers. One of them, a biker with flaming red hair, let out a low whistle at the sight of Kaylie.

"Is she new? Man, put me on the list for some of that."

One of the other bikers, the other one with spiky black hair who often trailed her, elbowed him in the side. Hard. It looked like it hurt. Devlin walked past them, ignoring them completely.

"Ow man, what the fuck? I was just saying I'd be down for sloppy seconds."

"Not this one. Just shut up."

Kaylie wasn't sure what she'd just overheard. Devlin didn't seem too concerned as they walked down a short slope to a flat barbecue area near the lake with about twenty picnic tables. It was meant for families most likely but the entire area was completely over run with bikers. Then again, Kaylie saw a few kids running around here and there. Bikers had families too.

She grinned a little bit at the incongruous sight of a huge tattooed man in leather lifting a little girl in a ballerina costume onto his shoulders. As soon as the man saw Devlin and her, he walked over. In fact, it seemed like everyone started to come over. They were swarmed in minutes as people approached to give Devlin their respects.

"This must be Kaylie. I'm Bob and this is Sally. Congrats on graduating, honey."

The big man held out a beefy hand. Kaylie shook it shyly before reaching up and shaking the adorable little girls hand, making her giggle.

He'd told them about her. When?

People waited politely to meet her and to bring Devlin and her drinks and food. She sipped a cold beer as she watched the bikers pull glass beer bottles from a row of stocked coolers. Coolers that sat right underneath a sign that said 'no glass containers.'

She had to laugh. The MC certainly did not follow the rules. But they did come up and introduce themselves, one by one. She finally met the big biker with long curly hair, Jack. He was Devlin's second in command. Then there was Donahue with merry blue eyes and black spiky hair, always hovering somewhere near Jack or Dav. She met Mike, also known as Whisky beard, one of the young prospects who she recognized from high school who had an angry red splotch on his cheek. There were too many other names to remember them all. She hoped she'd get the hang of it eventually.

Eventually. Everything about this felt like he was interested in being her boyfriend. Did bikers even date? She decided not to worry about it. Not yet.

In the midst of the introductions Kaylie noticed that at least a few people were less than enthusiastic about Devlin's arrival with her. The red haired biker seemed to be annoyed about the scenario. But it wasn't him that set off alarm bells in Kaylie's head.

Two women stood off to the side. Both were blond and attractive. One of the women was in her 30's but the other one looked only a couple of years older than Kaylie. Long blond hair, peachy skin, and a body that looked like she could moonlight as a swimsuit model. She would have been stunning if not for the pinched look on her face. For a moment Kaylie wondered what was wrong with her. Until she realized what is was. A heavy feeling settled in the pit of her stomach.

Oh. She was jealous.

Kaylie wondered if the girl had been Devlin's girlfriend before her. Maybe he ran through girls like tissue paper. Maybe she was being taken advantage of. She felt herself getting quiet, letting the conversations around her wash over her like water.

"Let's take a walk."

She looked up at him and nodded. Devlin pulled her out of the crowd to a path that circled the lake.

"Okay Kaylie, what's bothering you?"

He didn't sound mad, she realized thankfully. But he was throwing her off balance. He really did not beat around the bush did he? Well, then she wouldn't either.

"I'm not sure what I'm doing here."

"You're going for a walk. After that you are going to a picnic and after that, you are going to a carnival."

She stopped walking and gave him an exasperated look. He just grinned at her. The man was far too pleased with himself.

"Yes, but why?"

"Because you graduated."

"But why am I here *with you?*"

He gave her a knowing look and leaned back against a tree, crossing his arms.

"Don't tell me you don't know."

"I'm not being coy Devlin. I know you like me. I just don't know how many other girls get the royal treatment. There was a blond back there giving me evil looks. I don't want to step on someone else's territory."

He laughed.

"You are definitely not coy. Yes, I like you. No, there aren't any other girls. And no one has ever gotten the royal treatment before you. *Ever.*"

She narrowed her eyes at him, undecided.

"Come here, Kaylie."

She stayed where she was, lifting her chin. He laughed again and was on her in a second, lifting her up and over his shoulder like she weighed less than a rag doll. He carried her back to the tree and leaned her against the rough bark. Then he leaned over her, boxing her in with his arms.

Her breath was coming fast and shallow as he leaned forward with a heavy lidded look in his eyes. She looked away, suddenly nervous. He lifted her chin with one hand, forcing her to meet his eyes. What she saw there took her breath away. He wanted her. Even more than she realized. It was written all over his face.

"I know what I want and I go after it. I don't lie and I don't cheat. I'll take care of you if you let me Kaylie."

Her mouth opened slightly at his proclamation.

"Are you asking me to be your girlfriend?"

He just grinned and leaned forward, his mouth less than an inch from her ear.

"I'm asking for a little more than that. I play for keeps."

"Oh."

Her whole body was tingling from his nearness. She was trembling a little bit she realized. She hoped he didn't notice. He kissed her ear and then moved below it, nuzzling her neck deliciously with his soft lips.

"So?"

"What?"

Her voice sounded breathy, a ridiculous caricature of a woman in the throws of lust. He kept kissing her neck, working back up to her ear.

"Is the answer yes?"

She could barely think but she managed to get out a shaky nod and a whispered yes. He was staring down at her with a triumphant look on his face.

"Good. Because I wouldn't have left you alone anyway."

She should have been annoyed at his cockiness but she wasn't. Instead it sounded like an oath of something.

Something deep and true.

They both moaned as their lips met. He was finally kissing her, their breath commingling as they grasped each other desperately. He lifted her slightly, pushing her back into the tree trunk and pressing his body against hers. She gasped at the feeling of his hardness pressing into her belly. Oh god, he wanted to...

He was laughing again as he pulled away, stroking her hair gently. He lifted his body away from the intimate position they'd been in. She sighed as he broke contact, wanting him back against her almost immediately.

"No Kaylie I'm not going to try to do *that* in a public park."

"I knew that."

"Did you?"

She just stared at him, hoping her breath would return to normal, hoping she'd get used to the whirlwind of emotions he created in her so easily. It was annoying, how easy it was for him to turn her upside down. She decided it was important for her peace of mind that he didn't know the full extent of the control he had over her body and senses.

Because if he knew, who knew what he would do?

5

Devlin stared down at Kaylie. He was sorely tempted to find a private place to continue what they'd started but he put it out of his mind. He knew he wouldn't go through with it anyway. Kaylie was not the sort of girl you took in a parking lot. She still looked concerned, even though he'd kissed her senseless less than a minute before.

"Any other questions for me sweetheart?"

"Yes. I mean, just one."

"Go ahead."

"Why me? It can't just be my-"

He grinned and raised an eyebrow. "Your charms?"

She nodded sheepishly. Her charms were exceptional and certainly part of the reason he'd been drawn to her. But that wasn't why he'd first noticed her. In fact, he had started going to the diner because of Johnny.

"That's part of it. You are incredibly beautiful Kaylie."

She looked doubtful at that. He tried not to laugh again. His girl was sheer perfection. Beautiful but not vain, naturally sexy without any artifice or vulgarity. She deserved a real answer though, not flattery. He took a deep breath, hoping she wouldn't take this the wrong way.

"It started with Johnny."

"Johnny? The little boy who-"

He nodded. Johnny was mentally disabled. Sweet kid, industrious, even had a paper route. But he was special, and he'd had a hard time of it with the other kids making fun of him. The trouble was, he was just smart enough to *know* he was different. That was the hardest part.

"Johnny was always talking about this pretty girl who gave him an extra scoop of ice cream at Mae's. The kid loved going to that place. He even got a second job mowing lawns so he could afford to go in twice a week."

"He was a sweet boy. All I did was talk to him."

"It meant a lot to him Kaylie. So after he died I went in there to have his favorite. In his honor."

She smiled sadly.

"Banana split with extra nuts."

"Right. And then this stunningly beautiful girl walks over and takes my order. I couldn't believe there was an angel like you in this town. I knew I had to make you mine."

"Me? You are joking right?"

"Do I seem like I'm joking?"

She stared up at him and he raised his eyebrow as he smiled at her. She blushed immediately which made him smile even wider.

"Unfortunately, you were a little too young for me. So I had to wait."

"I still don't understand. Did Johnny come around the clubhouse or something?"

"Yeah, he hung out there a lot. Johnny was my brother."

Her sweet little mouth dropped open and a look of concern replaced the disbelief that had been there a moment before.

"I'm so sorry Devlin. I didn't know. We were all so sad about what happened to him. Oh god-"

She stared at him, finally putting the pieces together. Johnny and his mother had died in a car accident. That meant...

"You lost your mother too... Oh god, I'm so sorry."

He smiled at her softly. He really appreciated her words of condolence. They meant something.

"Thank you."

"So that's why you came in every week?"

"I had to check up on you and see how you were doing. I kept hoping you'd give me an extra scoop of ice cream but you never did."

He looked so sad for a minute that she laughed. A serious look came over her face. It looked like the disbelief was back.

"You've been waiting this whole time? That was almost two years ago!"

He shook his head. He wasn't going to lie to her. She didn't need to know how many girls he'd had, or how many offers he'd turned down, including a couple of girls who'd wanted to fool around last night at the clubhouse after he'd dropped her off.

"I'm not a monk Kaylie. But I will be true to you."

She looked thoughtful for a minute. So she wasn't going to raise a fuss about all the other women. And there had been a lot. That was a relief. There was no way to explain that away, even to an innocent like Kaylie.

"Okay. I will be true too."

He laughed and she slapped his shoulder.

"What's so funny?"

"Nobody would try it sweetheart, no matter how much they wanted to."

She blushed, clearly understanding what he was saying to her. Nobody messed with Devlin or his riders.

"Come on, let's get something to eat."

6

Kaylie licked the hot sauce off her fingers and leaned back on the blanket that had magically appeared for them. So had two full plates of food along with two frosty cold beer bottles. She was already getting used to that. All the little things the people in the club did for Devlin. It wasn't just the club members, it was the prospects, the girlfriends, the hanger ons. Even the older generations were represented and went out of their way for Devlin. It really was a family picnic. And they all looked up to *him*.

Devlin was beside her, nursing his beer. He had been sipping the same bottle for at least an hour. She knew it was for her benefit. He wouldn't drink and drive with her on the back of his bike.

Things were definitely going better since their talk. Kaylie was finally relaxing and just enjoying herself. She hadn't seen the blond girl anywhere either. Maybe she had been imagining the girl's animosity. She was probably just a hanger on after all. There were a lot of sexy looking girls hanging around who didn't seem attached to anyone. A few were oiling themselves up and laying out in the sun to tan, but it was obviously just a ploy to get one of the guys to notice them. It probably worked. They were putting on quite a display. Devlin never once looked over there though. He was a gentleman through and through underneath all that leather.

Kaylie smiled to herself, wondering how Devlin would react to seeing her in her bikini. It was a little small on her truth be told. After all, the last time she'd had need of a bikini she'd been 15 years old and working at a summer camp during the day. She had definitely filled in since then. A lot.

But the lake looked inviting on such a warm day. It had been ages since she'd gone swimming. Besides, it would be extremely interesting to see if Devlin liked what he saw... She decided that she might as well go for it before she lost her nerve. She pulled her top off over her head in a fluid motion and got to her feet.

"What are you-"

"Swimming silly. Don't you want to come?"

She shimmied her cut off shorts down over her hips and smiled over her shoulder at him. The poor man looked thunderstruck as she laughed and ran towards the water. She'd never seen him looking anything but self assured. She doubted anyone ever had. He was the one sitting on the throne after all. He'd been born and bred to lead. He'd been the President since coming of age five years ago. Everyone knew that.

She ran into the water and dove in, ignoring the hooting and hollering all around her. The crowd of bikers had gone crazy as she dashed toward the sand, turning her cheeks bright pink. She came up gasping for air from the sudden chill. The water was way colder than she'd expected it to be! All the sudden she felt arms close around her and turned, sputtering with indignation.

Devlin smiled down at her, his wet hair curling over his forehead.

"You didn't think I was going to let you go in by yourself looking like that did you?"

She smiled at him.

"A lot of the girls are wearing bikinis."

He smiled and lifted her up before tossing her into the water a few feet away. She grabbed his ankle playfully under the water until he yanked her up into his arms again.

"Yeah but not one of them looks even remotely like you do. Jesus woman!"

"You're the one who told me to wear a bikini."

"I'm a genius."

"Well, you are smarter than you look..."

He growled at her as she pushed off and swam deeper from the shore. They didn't notice the eyes watching them from across the lake.

****

Dani was pouting as she watching Devlin and his new tramp frollicking in the water. He'd never acted that way with her. All he'd done was crook his finger when he wanted to fool around and pretty much ignored her the rest of the time.

But oh my, he'd been amazing in bed. She'd had plenty of guys before and since of course. None had come even close to matching Dev. Damn him and his sudden interest in relationships.

She'd known this was coming of course. Everyone had known that Devlin had a special lady in mind and was waiting until she was of age. But she hadn't imagined the hot slice of jealousy that would rip through her guts at the sight of them together.

Why hadn't he been that way with *her?*

"What'd you want to see me about Dani?"

She turned at the sound of Officer Grant's gravelly voice behind her. She flared her eyes at him coquettishly and he narrowed his, looking her over.

He'd asked her out before so she knew he liked what he saw. So far she had yet to give into his attentions.

"You're always saying how you wanted to put him away. Well, so do I."

"Oh really? How the tides have turned."

"Office Grant I have *always* been on the right side of the law!"

He grinned and stepped forward, grabbing her hips.

"I'd rather have you under it."

She giggled nervously. He was a little bit too aggressive for her taste. But if she had to give in to get what she wanted, so be it.

"That can be arranged."

He grunted and kissed her mouth hard. Then he lifted his head up and looked around making sure nobody could see them. He grabbed her hand and yanked her back towards a copse of trees and bushes.

Oh crap.

Dani's plan was to cause Devlin and his new hussy some trouble. Not to get mauled by Officer Friendly in the bushes. The last thing she needed was to get poison ivy on her ass.

"Um… Grant? What is your plan exactly?"

He turned once they were screened from the rest of the camp grounds and grinned at her, reaching for his belt buckle.

"I thought we'd kill two birds with one stone."

"Two birds?"

He nodded, his hands moving to his shirt buttons. Once they were undone, he reached for her.

"Uh huh. One bird is getting me laid. The other bird is getting Dev thrown in jail. And you're going to help me with that. Don't scream if I get a little rough. It's just for effect. Your job is make sure someone sees you guys together later tonight."

Her eyes widened as she took in his meaning. He ripped her shirt off, scratching her skin. Dani had to bite her lip to keep from whimpering as he forced her onto the ground.

7

Devlin was letting himself be led around the State Fair like a dog on a leash, but he didn't care. Kaylie's enthusiasm for the carnival was contagious. He realized he'd been smiling non stop while his woman dragged him onto various rides and fed him little bits of cotton candy.

Until he'd noticed her. The girl with long blond hair was following them.

Dani.

A couple of years ago he'd had a thing with Dani. Nothing serious, just fooled around a couple of times. She was a good looking girl but her attitude was always out of control and her mood swings made her not a lot of fun to be around. She was the younger sister of one of the club's old lady's so he couldn't just ignore her until she went away when he was done with her like he usually did with women. He'd had to sit down and have a talk with her about why it wasn't going to work out.

Hell, they'd just been kids. It was never going to 'work out' for them anyway. But Dani hadn't taken it well. And she hadn't given up hope. He'd never had a girlfriend in all the time since. Lots of girls had helped him pass the time but never for long. She hadn't much liked any of those girls either.

But this was different. He wouldn't let her intimidate his woman, or ruin even a second of her celebration today. Kaylie had already mentioned a blond girl staring at her. It would not make her happy if she found out Dani was his ex, or that she'd been trailing them all night. He would do anything to protect Kaylie, even if he had to tell Dani to back off and risk offending Bruce and his old lady Janine.

It didn't make sense though. Dani had to have known about Kaylie for a while now, everyone in the club did. He'd been having the guys look after her for so long now, it was hardly a secret what his intentions were. So acting surprised and jealous seemed way out of line. But there Dani was, stalking them like a jealous exgirlfriend. Which she hadn't been. Not really. He frowned as he followed Kaylie into the fun house, catching a flash of blond hair behind them. He could tell she'd been crying.

Damn it.

Thankfully Jack and Donahue were with them at the moment. He jerked his head backwards and whispered.

"Get rid of her."

Jack was gone in an instant, leaving Donahue to trail them through the fun house. Kaylie was laughing as a clown jumped out at them. He slipped his arm around her and used the scare as an opportunity to kiss her neck.

Hmmmm... he was going to have a hard time waiting to take her. Even if he knew he'd have her in his bed within the hour, it would be a painful wait. But he had promised himself (and her mother in less explicit terms) that he wouldn't take her for at least a week. She deserved that at the very least. She was a complete innocent as far as he could tell. He had to make sure that she was sure before he convinced her to lay down with him. That part would be easy. Getting his body to hold off for release was something else entirely.

He could ease into it though, take things a bit farther every night. He grinned at the thought, planning explicitly what he would do each night, and where. Only five more nights to go.

****

Kaylie inhaled as Devlin's hand closed over her breast. They were on the swing in the playground across the street from her house, hidden from view from the high fence. They'd been kissing for a half hour at least when he started sliding his hands over her body, getting more and more intimate with each pass.

She was surprisingly relaxed about kissing Devlin. He still made her head spin, but she wasn't terrified of doing it wrong, like she had been the first few times. She swirled her tongue against his playfully, eliciting a low growl from his throat. She was starting to get used to his sounds. He made the sexiest little noises when he was kissing her. And now that his hands were wandering his breathing was getting raspy.

His hand disappeared and a finger replaced it, tracing the outline of her nipple which was poking through her bikini and thin cotton top. Her sweater must have fallen off... or more likely, he had pushed it off to get better access to her. A strange feeling was coursing through her body, centering in between her legs. This was more intense than the other times. He wasn't being playful now. He was serious.

She gasped as he pinched her nipple lightly. He laughed throatily, resting his forehead on hers.

"Oh so you like that do you?"

She didn't trust herself to speak while he traced the collar of her blouse, dipping his finger inside to pull on her bikini strap. His other hand reached around her and pulled her tightly against him. Against the burning heat of his erection.

Oh god...

He pulled her top down and to the side, then pushed the triangle of her bikini top covering her breast aside. Suddenly she was completely bare to him. He moaned and lowered his head to her chest, suckling her nipple lightly.

She felt herself slipping backwards in his embrace as her hands wound through his hair, clasping his head closer to her. He moaned and rocked his hips gently into hers rhythmically. He pulled her top down on the other side and started kissing her other breast. Now he was alternating back and forth, using his hands and tongue to tweak her nipples, driving her insane with desire.

They were both making soft guttural sounds as he guided her legs around his waist, bringing her feminity into direct contact with... him. They were practically lying down on the swing she realized. It was a good thing it was dark out!

"Damn... we better stop."

Kaylie felt dazed as he pulled her into a sitting position and adjusted her top back into place. He was breathing heavily and looked strange. As if he was concentrating on something. Or in pain.

"Are you alright?"

"Yeah, I'm- Don't look at me like that Kaylie. Please... oh god."

He pulled her back into his arms and kissed her deeply. She forget everything for a moment. Who she was, where she was, who he was to her... If he had wanted to take her then and there, she would have let him.

He let out a muffled curse as he forcefully lifted her to her feet, placing her at arms length from his body. She chewed her lip and stepped toward him.

He laughed harshly.

"Sweetheart, trust me, you do not want to get close to me right now."

"Why not?"

He gave her a wry smile, before his eyes shifted to her heaving bosom. He closed his eyes and held her shoulders so she wouldn't come any closer.

"Because that's not how this is going to happen."

"What?"

"Your first time."

"Oh."

He had a sudden thought and looked at her almost hopefully.

"It will be your first time, won't it Kaylie? Because if not..."

She was tempted to lie to him if it would get him to kiss her again. But she wouldn't do that. Besides, he'd find out soon enough. She felt her cheeks turning pink at the thought. She wanted him to take her. She wanted him.

Badly.

"I'm sorry… I've never… been with anyone else."

He just stared at her, the look in his eyes making her shiver.

"Did I do something wrong? Maybe you don't want to be with someone as inexperienced as me."

He groaned and pulled her into his arms, kissing her hungrily. Then he pushed her away again.

"No Kaylie. Trust me, that's not a problem. You are perfect."

She smiled up at him, feeling reassured. She took another step in, hoping he'd kiss her like that again. He laughed and gave her a gentle little shove, pushing her toward the street.

"And now you better take that sweet perfection inside."

She pouted and looked over her shoulder at him. He just stared at her.

"Go on."

"Goodnight Devlin."

"Goodnight Kaylie."

8

He saw her every night that week, even on the nights she worked at Mae's. He'd come in for a banana split, just like Johnny used to like. She made sure to give him an extra scoop as a sign of her affection, which made him grin. It was always toward the end of her shift when he'd come strolling into Mae's, looking like a hawk in a dovecote. Then he'd wait at the counter until she was ready to go home. They would find a quiet spot to talk and fool around for a couple of hours. Her mother was always up reading when she got home, with no recriminations. Even she trusted Dev with her daughter. If only she knew that it was Kaylie who was starting to get impatient. She wanted the real thing.

She was ready.

When she said goodnight to him on Thursday he was quiet, grim even. They'd gone further than ever before.

She'd even touched him there- through his pants. He'd felt so big and warm- dangerously powerful but also- so tempting and exciting. She kissed his cheek while he stared at her darkly, biking off as soon as the front door was closed, without the final wave that he usually gave her.

Little did she know, that was the last she would see of him for 48 hours. He didn't visit her the next night at Mae's during her shift, or call. There was a bike parked outside the whole night though she knew it wasn't his. She was already learning to recognize which ride belonged to who. When she finally closed up it was Jack who followed her home. He didn't offer her a ride or an explanation. As usual, all he did was nod.

Kaylie wasn't sure why Devlin was staying away from her, but she felt awful about it. Her insides felt like they were hollow, empty. Maybe she should have let him do more. He hadn't pushed her but maybe she had missed a cue from lack of experience. He must be bored with a virgin. Maybe he didn't want her anymore...

She cried into her pillow for hours, tossing and turning. She made sure her light was out so when her mother came in to say goodnight, she wouldn't notice her red eyes or tear stained cheeks. It was near dawn by the time Kaylie fell into a fitful sleep.

It was the longest night of her life.

Devlin was in hell. It was ironic that someone with the nickname of 'Devil' would end up in hell. Even more surprising was that he was loving every minute of it. Well, not every minute. Not the past two days.

Kaylie was driving him insane. He'd seen her every night this week and every night he'd dared to go a little further with her. But once he'd opened pandora's box, she was the one who didn't want to stop. He grimaced, just thinking about what she'd done to him two nights ago... once again leaving him with an uncomfortable erection.

He'd even stayed away last night to see if he could loosen her hold on him. He was the one who'd drank beer after beer, staring miserably at the clock, counting the hours until he could see her again. It was happening so fast- this feeling that he wasn't just him anymore- now he was part of an 'us.' It wasn't even just wanting her, thought that was a big part of it. He didn't feel like he was in control of his feelings anymore. He didn't like it.

Two nights ago they'd been fooling around for an hour, he'd finally touched her between her legs, over her tight denim shorts. He'd been wondering about the wisdom of unzipping her shorts when he'd felt her tentative caress on the front of his jeans. Jesus. That fluttering little touch had almost sent him over the edge. And then she'd gotten bolder.

He'd had to take another cold shower last night. He was enjoying her, more than he thought was possible, but his patience was wearing thin.

Tonight was the night. He was done waiting, and if he were honest with himself, she seemed to be done waiting too.   If he could just get through this meeting he'd be fine. He was finding him mind was less focused than usual. He forced himself to listen careful to what Jack was reporting. The new Sheriff was making things difficult for the club. They already knew that. But now it was looking like his animosity was specifically targeted at Devlin.

He'd been ticketed again last night, after he'd dropped off Kaylie thankfully. He didn't want to think about giving the cops a chance to hassle his woman. She was so delicate... he frowned at the thought of upsetting her. Enough was enough.

"This stops now. Find out what they have on me. You still in with your cousin, Donnie?"

Donahue nodded. His cousin was on the force one town over. He couldn't keep the cops off their asses but he could tip them off when a big bust was brewing. The Spawns of Satan, also known as the SOS, didn't officially traffic in drugs, guns or hookers, but they did have their own set of laws. And they did *partake* in drugs, guns and hookers. Well not Dev, but a lot of the guys did. He didn't enjoy drugs because of his need for control and he never needed to pay for sex. In fact, he spent most of his time turning women down.

It was a running joke at the clubhouse that Dev had the best sloppy seconds. Girls just hung around waiting for him to notice them all the time. If he did, he didn't usually see them more than once. When he passed them over, they became easy pickings for the rest of the guys in the club. He couldn't tell you the number of times he'd been credited with getting another Spawn laid. For the most part, Devlin ignored it. Sex was just sex. He saw no need to talk about it.

Being good looking was definitely part of it, but it was the power of running the SOS that had made it go over the top. He was bored by it. He knew what he wanted and he'd found it. His mind wandered back to Kaylie and what they'd be doing later tonight. He couldn't wait to make her his once and for all.

He had to take care of this cop situation so it didn't blow back on her. Once people knew she was his old lady, she'd be affected by everything he did. Speaking of which, Jack hadn't had an easy time getting rid of Dani the other night at the State Fair. She'd resisted his guttural demand to vacate the carnival apparently. He'd had to use some rough moves on her to get her to leave. He hadn't hurt her, Dev wouldn't stand for that, but it hadn't been pretty. Dev was pretty sure they should expect more trouble from Dani, brother in law in the Club or not.

"Okay find out what's up. And get Bruce in here. I need to talk to him about his sister in law."

"Dani?"

"Yeah."

He drummed his fingers on the heavy wood table. The meeting room was large enough to accommodate the core members of the club, but they were growing. They also had a couple of other smaller clubs that were part of a larger circle, counting themselves as unofficial members of the SOS. Kind of like cousins.

Things were changing. Someone had even mentioned changing the name of the Club from Spawns of Satan to Devil's Riders. He didn't mind being called Devil but naming the club after him seemed like a slap in the face to the old timers. To his own father and grandfather who'd started the club. He could picture them rolling over in their graves at the thought. Devil's Riders was fine as a nickname but that was it. Still, he couldn't help but notice how many people had started using it.

Bruce walked in and sat down at the table with Dev and Jack. Donnie shut the heavy wood door and leaned against it. Devlin stared at Bruce for a couple of minutes before starting. The older club member looked nervous which was pretty funny considering the guy was a 6'4" wall of muscle and had been in and out prison most of his adult life. He'd calmed down in his mid thirties after getting hitched and was spending less and less time at the clubhouse these days. It was a good thing he'd been there tonight or they would have had to call him in. Who knows how long that would have taken.

"Thanks for coming Bruce. I need to talk to you about your sister in law."

Bruce nodded.

"Dani's been out of control lately. I heard about what happened at the carnival, man. I'm sorry."

"Can you get her to chill out?"

He shook his head.

"I haven't seen her all week, man. I can definitely try but the problem's not just her. It's my old lady too. They are both in a tizzy about your new girl. Calling her an interloper. Saying she's friends with cops."

"She went to high school with a few of the newer cops but that's it. Hell, she went to school with whisky beard too. It doesn't matter anyway. Kaylie is my old lady now. She's off limits to this kind of bullshit."

"Congrats Dev. I didn't know that."

Dev nodded.

"Okay, you need to get your old lady in line. I won't tell you how to do it. Rip up her credit cards or something. If she or Dani come near Kaylie again they will be banned from the club house. Permanently."

Bruce inhaled sharply but nodded. He knew the drill. Dev put Dani and the club out of his mind as the older man left. He was grinning when Donnie handed him a beer.

"No thanks man. I have a date tonight."

Donnie rolled his eyes at him.

"Yeah, we know."

"Did you get the cabin aired out?"

"Yeah, man it's full of fucking rose petals too."

"Very funny. See you tomorrow my brothers."

He clasped their hands and strode out of the club house. It was time to go and get his woman.

9

Kaylie knew something was up. Devlin had shown up tonight as if nothing had happened between them. He seemed tense, and offered no explanation for staying away the night before. She decided not to ask, knowing that if he was here now, whatever was bothering him had nothing to do with her, or he'd resolved it on his own.

It might have only been a week that they'd spent together, but she'd been observing him covertly for the past few years. At least when he came into the diner anyway. Apparently, he'd been observing her too. Everywhere. She knew he was fiercely independent and tended to do things on his own, though always with the club at his back. She was already attuned to his mood shifts. He wasn't a talker, or morose, but he his emotions ran deep, particularly where she was concerned.

He was definitely still worried about something, she could tell. It was obvious from the moment he arrived to pick her up. She hurried out to the bike and slid her arms around his neck. He smiled and kissed her before pulling her onto the bike. He was in a hurry to leave.

They were off and running the moment she had her arms around his waist. As usual he didn't tell her where they were going. And as usual, she didn't mind. Judging from this week, she'd been taken to scenic spots and a few bar-b-q's, even one home cooked meal at his Aunt Edna's house. His folks were gone so she knew it was the equivalent of meeting the parents.

Things were moving fast. Really fast. Kaylie was surprised that she didn't mind. In fact, she wanted to go faster.

Dating a biker was bringing out all sorts of surprising personality traits in her.

No, they weren't dating. It was more than that. They'd skipped all the courtship, although she supposed he'd been courting in his own way by looking out for her and coming into Mae's all those years.

They weren't dating. They were *together.*

The thought sent a warm feeling shooting through her insides. She knew she was in danger of falling in love. It wasn't that she didn't trust him. She did, she trusted him implicitly in fact. But it was too soon. She was afraid that she'd make a fool of herself or say something she couldn't take back. He stole all thought from her when he was touching her. And he'd been touching her a lot more lately...

She sighed and looked out at the woods. They'd never gone this way before. He was taking the road toward Heller Mountain. She snuggled into his back and promised herself to keep her mouth shut about her feelings.

Bikers didn't care about love anyway. He might want her close at hand but she couldn't imagine him professing his love for her. Neither one of them were much for words. It was one of the reasons they were so well suited. Telling him that she loved him would only ruin things.

And right now, everything was perfect. Maybe he'd tell her what was bothering him tonight. But if he didn't, she wouldn't ask. She couldn't risk it.

****

Devlin pulled up the cabin after a leisurely 45 minute drive. He always went about 20 MPH slower when Kaylie was on the back of his bike. But even when he wasn't, he found himself being a bit more careful on the road. He had someone now. His devil may care attitude was shifting. He frowned, not sure he liked the change.

Devil's weren't supposed to be cautious. He shook off the feeling of foreboding that was coming over him. Tonight he would finally get what he wanted. He'd never waited for anything this long before in his life. His fingers itched to touch her skin as he parked and dismounted. Kaylie must have sensed his mood because she was quiet as he pulled off her helmet and led her to the front porch.

He fished around for the hidden key and unlocked the door. He flipped on a light and guided Kaylie inside. The cabin was rustic but clean. A frequent hide out for anyone in the SOS who needed to lie low, it had been in Dev's family since the 1950's. Other than that, his folks had brought him out here for vacations when he was kid. Now it was mostly unused.

She looked around her, taking it in. "What is this place?"

"My Grandfather built it. Do you like it?"

She nodded her head but didn't say anything else. He could tell she was overwhelmed. Whether by the cabin itself, or the prospect of spending the night alone with him, he wasn't sure. He took her hand and pulled her to the back of the house.

"Come on, let me show you the best part."

There was a screen door that led to a back porch. He pushed it open and Kaylie made a sweet surprised gasp. The sun was setting over the small lake. It was unbelievably private. A tire swing hung on a tree branch, dangling over the water.

"It's beautiful!"

He smiled at the rapturous expression on her face.

"The view's even better from in here."

He took her back inside and up a flight of stairs into a large bedroom. He pulled her into his arms. He couldn't wait any longer. He needed her. He needed to forget the world and lose himself in her sweetness. She was looking down at his chest, looking very nervous suddenly. He licked his lips and lowered his head. He knew how to make her relax... how to drive her wild.

He took his time kissing her, using his mouth alone. After a while he pulled her closer to him, sliding his hands up and down her delicious back to cup her sweetly rounded bottom. When he pressed her against the hardness in his pants she sighed audibly. He groaned as he resisted the urge to grind himself into her softness. There was no need to rush. He'd told her mother she'd be home by dawn. They had all night. And he intended to use it.

****

Devlin was unbuttoning her blouse while he nibbled on her earlobes. Her sudden shyness was evaporating, just as the certainty that he was going to finally make love to her tonight was setting in. She had a general idea of the mechanics involved in sex, just none of the specifics. Thankfully Dev seemed to know exactly what he was doing.

Her breath was coming in little pants as he slid her blouse off and over her shoulders. He groaned as his hands closed over her thin cotton bra. He caressed her gently, kissing her mouth again before she felt him unhook her bra behind her. As soon as her bra was off everything changed. He stared down at her naked chest for a moment with an absorbed look on his face. Then he went wild. His hands were everywhere and his mouth- oh, his mouth was everywhere too. He lavished her breasts with attention endlessly before scooping her up and laying her on the bedspread. Then he pulled his shirt off and pressed himself against her.

Oh god-

The heat of his chest felt incredible against her breasts and stomach. He was kissing her again as he rocked his hips into hers. There was no doubt now. That's what he wanted to do.

She wanted to do it too.

She didn't protest when his fingers found the button on her denim shorts. He deftly undid them and pushed them down over her hips, taking her panties part of the way so that her body was barely covered at all. He leaned back and pulled her shorts off of her legs. Then he settled between her legs, slowly tracing his finger along the top edge of her panties while she waited breathlessly to see what he would do. He was staring at her junction with a heavy lidded look in his eyes. Heat radiated from his hands where they rested on her hips.

Finally he moved, one hand hovering over her mound. She shivered as he began lightly touching her through her panties, making small circles over her femininity before retreating. Then he began again, slowly teasing her until she was writhing on the bed. The weight of his legs pressed down on hers, holding her in place as her hips bucked slowly. Finally he leaned forward, kissing her as he used his other hand to pull her panties down and away.

Now his hand was on her bare skin, playing with the soft folds between her legs. She felt so warm down there... and surprisingly slick.

"Jesus Kaylie..."

She couldn't think straight as he brought her closer and closer to the edge, without letting her fall over it. Finally he pulled away and she watched as he pulled his jeans off and threw them aside. He was so beautiful... and big. Oh dear god, he was big.

Devlin's shaft stood straight up from his narrow hips, reaching nearly to his belly button. A small fearful gasp escaped her lips and he was back in an instant, kissing and soothing her.

"It's alright Kaylie. I promise."

She nodded but her body had gone stiff. The heat between her legs was still there but the rest of her was running for the hills, tensed up and prepared for pain.

"Shhhhh sweetheart, don't be afraid of me."

His soft words combined with his skillful hands started to relax her again as he slid his finger up and down the line between her nether lips. He wasn't pushing himself inside her or doing anything except kissing and touching her. Her body started to respond again, hovering on the edge of release.

"Oh!"

He suckled her nipples as his finger started to strum the tender nub above her opening. He slipped a slender finger inside her as she felt herself start to climax for the first time.

"Oh, oh, oh, OH!"

She hardly recognized the high pitched breathy sounds she was making as the world seemed to explode around her. Her body would have lifted off the bed entirely if he hadn't been lying partially on top of her. As she floated back to earth she felt him adjusting his weight as he positioned himself between her legs.

"Kaylie, look at me."

She opened her eyes with an effort and stared up at Devlin. The mysterious man she felt like she'd known forever. That she'd wanted forever... She nodded, giving him permission to move forward. She didn't care about the pain anymore.

She gasped with pleasure as he pushed the tip of his manhood against her opening. He was hard as a rock against her softness, but also silky... and incredibly hot. He pressed forward a few inches and just like that, he was inside her.

Ohhhh...

It felt good. Really good. He flexed his hips and the angle changed. She felt him slip deeper inside her. Her body felt stretched open and utterly exposed. But she knew he wouldn't hurt her. She watched his face as he eased himself out and back in slowly. His eyes were closed and it looked like he was concentrating with every fiber of his being. She realized he was struggling to hold onto his control. She wondered if it felt as good to him as it did to her.

He groaned as he rocked himself back into her again, a little deeper this time. It hurt a little bit now, but it was commingled with the most exquisite pleasure she'd ever experienced before, or even imagined. He fit inside her perfectly, filling her with liquid heat.

The pressure was starting to build inside her again as he worked himself in and out of her gently, gaining greater access with each stroke. Where was the pain she was supposed to be experiencing? Where-

Ouch!

He bumped up against something and they both moaned. Her barrier was preventing him from penetrating her fully. He held perfectly still above her.

"Kaylie."

"Yes?"

"I'm going to take you now."

"Oh... I thought you already were."

He let out a shout of strangled laughter.

"No, not quite yet."

"Okay."

"Listen- I'm going to try not to hurt you- I can squeeze by without tearing anything- but- hmmmfff- you're so tight that it's harder than I thought it would be-"

He moaned as she clenched down on him instinctively. Her hips were making tiny circles against him subconsciously. He closed his eyes tightly and pushed forward. She felt the membrane inside her give way. She'd always imagined he would just tear through it forcefully. From what she'd heard that was what was normal. But he'd done it so gently that he was embedded inside her without more than the slightest discomfort.

"Unffff... Jesus Kaylie you feel... so good... are you alright sweetheart?"

"Uh huh- yes- just- can you-"

He swallowed as he stared down into her big brown eyes. She looked so sweet and trusting- and so fucking hot that he could barely stop himself from plunging into her honied depths.

"Yes?"

"Can you, oh! Can you... move like you were before?"

Relief and desire poured through him. He hadn't imagined he could be more turned on than he already was, but he'd been wrong. Her sweet admission that she wanted him to get on with it made him want to laugh and lose himself inside her all at once.

"Yes, I can do that."

He pressed a kiss into her lips before letting his body take over. He kept himself in control, not going too fast but not too slow either. He could hardly believe she was finally his after all this time. Her body had exceeded his wildest imaginings, the way she looked and oh god- the way she felt. Even after he'd seen her in that bikini he hadn't expected her to feel this good... her skin was like silk. She was firm and smooth and rounded in all the right places. He didn't think he would ever be able to get enough of her.

He groaned and picked up the tempo. He could feel her responding to him. She was so natural and beautiful. Her body knew what to do and she let it happen without shame or embarrassment. She might be shy but that just added to her appeal. He grunted as he felt her squeeze down on him. There was no way he could last much longer.

Then he remembered that this wasn't a one time thing, that she was his old lady now and he could have her again, maybe even tonight if she wasn't too sore. He'd never had that feeling before- for the first time in his life he wanted more and he knew he would have it. The thought of having her again sent him over the edge. His hips jerked spasmodically, as he felt himself explode inside her. He filled her with his seed, pumping himself out of tempo as her body clenched down on him, pulling him deeper...

He lay on top of her, trying to catch his breath, unable to think or move for a moment.

Jesus.

He'd never come so hard in his life. Whatever power Kaylie had over him, whatever time he'd put in to make sure her mother wouldn't object, that he was free from encumbrances, that she would trust him, it had all been worth it. He knew nobody would ever make him feel this way again.

She was his.

****

Kaylie was laughing as she ran up to the house in her wet skivvies. It was freezing in the mountains. Who ever had decided it was a good idea to jump in the lake was insane! Actually, once she thought about it, she realized it had been her idea... more or less. He'd dared to her to do it after she'd asked him if he ever swam in the lake. They'd been lying in bed together... after...

The whole evening had been a blur. Making love. He'd held her for a long while afterwards. They'd had something to eat and then decided to skinny dip in the dark- well almost skinny dipping. She'd left her bra and panties on. She wasn't that comfortable with him yet! Besides, what if someone walked in on them?

She giggled and slammed the door behind her, pretending to lock Devlin out. He was buck naked, since he had not been wearing anything under his jeans. He'd mumbled something about going commando when she blushed and looked away. She wondered if he'd been naked all those other times they'd fooled around... the thought made her feel a little bit weak in the knees.

Dev appeared at the locked screen door, pretending that he was going to break it down. He snarled like a dog and then yipped at her when she opened the door. She was still laughing when he scooped her up and carried her back to the bedroom.

"How do you feel?"

She slid her arms around his neck. His muscled chest felt so warm. He looked so damn sexy!

"Good."

"Good?"

"Very, very good."

He brushed a strand of wet hair away from her face.

"I didn't hurt you?"

She blushed and looked away, peeking back up at him.

"Just a little. I thought it was going to be much worse."

He grinned and lifted her into his arms, depositing her on the bed.

"I did some research into this. The whole virgin thing is a fallacy. There's a membrane but it doesn't have to tear, you just need to nudge it out of the way."

She stared up at him while he grabbed a towel and started rubbing her down.

"You did that? For me?"

He grinned and tossed the towel aside, pouncing on her.

"Well, not just for you. I sort of enjoyed it too."

"Sort of!"

She squealed indignantly as he grabbed her and rolled her towards him.

"More than sort of."

He kissed her mouth.

"More than a lot."

He kissed her ear.

"More than ever."

He kissed her neck and she sighed, knowing he was going to make love to her again. Knowing she would love every second of it.

10

Dev was focused intently on the road as he drove Kaylie home in the early morning light. It had started to drizzle and he wanted to be extra careful. His earlier concern about losing his daring was gone. She was precious. She was his. He had to keep her safe. And he would.

She'd made him feel things that night that surprised the hell out of him. He'd known she was special. He hadn't know how special she would make *him* feel. He was changing already and he'd just started falling for her. He's wanted her for a long time but loving her, that was different.

Fucking *love* man.

He didn't even cringe back from the word now, not after she'd given him everything. And she had. She'd held nothing back when she was in his arms. Being with her was unlike anything he'd ever experienced. He finally understood why people believed in all the fairy tale bullshit he'd scorned for so long.

He was going to marry her.

Jesus!

He almost skidded out as the cop lights came on behind him. The blaring siren sounded like it was less than ten feet away. Where the hell had that come from? They must have been waiting in the woods for him to come down this way. But how would they know that? And why were they ambushing him?

He felt Kaylie hands tighten around his stomach as he pulled to the side of the road. This was not good. Not good at all.

He turned off the bike and spoke in a low tone over his shoulder.

"Don't say anything. I'll take care of this."

He looked back to see that there were two cop cars back there. Great. Office Grant and Sheriff Dooley were walking toward him with their night sticks swinging. Shit. He might have to take some licks this time. As long as they didn't touch her...

"If they hit me, just get out of the way."

"What? No!"

"Kaylie, just do it damn it!"

"What do we have here Officer Grant?"

The mocking drawl of Sheriff Dooley filled Devlin with dread. He'd never feared the police. Not until tonight. He forced a placid expression on his face.

"How can I help you Sheriff?"

"Who's that you got with you Dev?"

He cringed as Grant looked Kaylie over, grinning widely.

"My old lady."

"You don't say. Hey, aren't you the cutie who works down at Mae's?"

He didn't have turn his head to see Kaylie was afraid of Grant. He could just feel it. He tried to switch their focus off of the terrified girl behind him and back onto the matter at hand. It was hard to keep the scorn from his voice but he managed it.

"What seems to be the problem Sheriff?"

"We were looking for you."

"I'm flattered."

"Don't be. We have reason to suspect that you are involved in a felony. The attack of a young woman."

"What?"

"I said, you are being charged with attacking a young woman."

Grant slapped his thigh, still leering at Kaylie. Devlin felt like his stomach was falling into his boots.

"Oooeeee, she's a looker. Or she was until you roughed her up. Not like this one though. You sure have good taste for an outlaw."

"I haven't *attacked* anyone."

"Well, see, she says you did. And you being who you are, doesn't seem so far fetched. Criminal element and what not."

"When did she say this happened?"

"Last Saturday at the State Fair."

"He was with me."

The Sheriff leaned down and peered at Kaylie. Devlin gritted his teeth.

"What's that miss?"

"I said, he couldn't have attacked anyone because he was with me."

The Sheriff gave her an appraising look.

"All day and all night?"

"Yes."

"Well be that as it may, I'm going to have to take him in for questioning. Stand up now please Mr. McRae and face the bike."

Devlin closed his eyes and forced himself to comply. The bastards were doing this out of spite. It was just scare tactics. He hadn't attacked anyone and they knew it. He just wished they had picked a time when Kaylie wasn't with him. Never mind that they were in the middle of nowhere.

He felt the cuffs snap closed around his wrists and turned around, careful not to make any sudden movements.

"We'll bring you back for your bike *if* the charges are dropped."

"Somebody has to come pick up Kaylie."

Grant slapped his knee.

"Kaylie! That's it. I knew it. You sure look all grown up don't you now, darlin'?"

Sheriff Dooley pulled Devlin away just as Grant put his arm over her shoulders solicitously. He looked her over and grinned at Devlin.

"Don't worry about a thing Mr. McRae. I'll see the little darlin' home."

He felt rage boiling up inside him as he was pushed into the back of the squad car. If he hadn't of been cuffed he would have killed the man. He still might.

He watched as Kaylie followed the officer to the second car. She made eye contact with him through the window, trying to reassure him. She looked scared.

"I'll go to the club house! Don't worry!"

He gritted his teeth as Grant opened the passenger side door for Kaylie. At least he wasn't making her ride in the back. But if he touched her... he leaned his forehead against the padded wall separating him from the front and silently screamed.

They held him for three days. Three awful days during which Kaylie imagined horrible things happening to him. Her mind went wild, picturing every scenario in the book. All except Dev being guilty. That never even crossed her mind.

She'd been true to her word, getting her mother to drive her to the clubhouse as soon as that disgusting Officer Grant had pulled away. The way he'd looked at her... and spoken to her... it was revolting. He'd acted as if she was easy, a woman of ill repute. He'd even implied that he'd make sure Dev got out if she'd 'make nice' with him. She'd had to fight back the bile rising in her throat at his lurid insinuations. But he hadn't touched her.

She'd kept herself focused by thinking about Dev and what she would say when she got to the clubhouse. She'd never been there before but she knew where it was. Everyone in town did, mostly just so they could steer clear of the place.

The building had been cleaner than she'd expected. That is until she got to the bar room. There were people everywhere, bikers mostly but also a lot of women in various states of undress. There were two stripper poles in the room and each had a girl hanging off of them, dancing lazily. Everyone in the room was drunk except her.

Donnie had seen her immediately and been across the room in two seconds flat.

"You shouldn't be here. Dev wouldn't like it."

"He's been arrested- they said-"

He'd held up a finger, silencing her.

"Come on, let's find Jack. You can tell us both."

They'd pulled her into a hallway and waited until there was a break in the traffic to and from the bathrooms. Then she heard Jack say the first words she'd ever heard him say.

"What happened?"

She'd told them everything. Halfway through the story Donnie looked at Jack and said one word.

"Dani."

Jack had nodded and just like that, Donnie was gone. Kaylie had started crying then. The tension and worry had finally gotten to her. She leaned against Jack's shoulder and cried all over his leather while he held perfectly still.

11

They had nothing on him. He knew that. Dev sat in the dim light on the uncomfortable bench making plans. No one had come to see him, but he knew they'd tried. They'd taunted him with that information.

'Your little honey was here today. She looked so sad when we told her you couldn't come out and play.'

He clenched his fists and got into position to do another set of push ups. He didn't even know who had accused him and of what exactly. He had a strong suspicion it was Dani. If they tried to prove that he'd laid a hand on her... they'd have a hard time doing that. Any member of the SOS would come forward and take the fall for him. That's if Dani actually had any physical evidence. The Spawns had an attorney on retainer. He was coming by later today. He was almost as pissed off as Devlin was.

It was pretty clear the cops were using the trumped up charges against him to try and aggravate him into attacking a police officer. That was an old school technique. Now they were using every trick in the book to drag out his stay. He'd come close to taking the bait more than once. Officer Grant had an annoying habit of stopping by the dank cell they were keeping him in and dropping hints about what he'd done, and what he'd like to do, to Kaylie.

'I can't wait to take a big bite of that honey pie. Does she squeal when you stick her? I bet I can make her squeal. Almost did the other night too.'

Then Grant had started making squealing noises every time he walked by, the bastard. It almost worked. Instead Dev had used his famous self control to do deep inside himself, to imagine the kinds of things he would do to Officer Grant if even one word he'd said was true. And a few things he would do to him just for thinking them. Officer

Grant's life was going to get very difficult from here on out. If he'd laid one finger on his woman though... he was in for the beating of a life time.

Violence was part of the MC life, but there was a time and a place for it. In this case he couldn't very well beat up an officer of the law, unless Grant didn't know for sure who was doing the beating. A bag over the head after a night out drinking was the easiest way. Hiring out was another. But Devlin wanted to be there. He wanted to hear the crunch when his fist connected with Grants big, fat mouth.

Simmering rage didn't come close to what he was feeling. The pot had long since boiled over and now he was just hot metal bouncing around on the stove.

Ready to burn someone.

****

Kaylie waited outside her house for her ride. Donnie had called her and said he was coming to pick her up, that Devlin was getting out. She felt elated momentarily before the worries started to set back in. She'd had a lot of time to think the past few days. She was starting to wonder if she'd let her heart get her into a situation she'd regret for the rest of her life.

She wasn't sure she was cut out to belong to a biker, let alone the President of the most notorious gang in Northern California. The thought of not being with him cut her deep inside. But the thought of being dragged through the mud over and over again was scaring the heck out of her. Even her mother was concerned, and she'd been firmly on Devlin's side since the beginning.

Donnie drove up in an SUV. She hadn't been expecting that. She climbed in and sat there nervously as Donnie turned off the radio and waited for her to put on her seatbelt. She'd dressed conservatively for the occasion in a simple navy dress with a pink cardigan and kitten heeled pumps. Her hair was down and she wore sunglasses. She didn't want Devlin to see the doubt in her eyes.

She knew the charges against him were false. He would never hurt a woman and he certainly wouldn't force himself on one. Why would he when every woman he came into contact with melted like butter? Including her.

Especially her.

The drive to the courthouse in the center of town seemed to last forever. And yet she was so nervous that she wished it took longer. Hours, not minutes. Days.

What would she say when she saw him?

****

Devlin stepped out into the sunlight. He'd finally been released on bail after hours of back and forth legal bullshit. His lawyer was still inside threatening to sue the department for harassment if they didn't drop the charges. He shielded his eyes. The bright light hurt his eyes after three days stuck in the dark cell. He was pretty sure they'd chosen the worst cell in the place. It sure didn't smell like it'd been cleaned in the last decade or so.

He inhaled deeply as he saw Kaylie climbing out of the SUV across the street. She turned toward the courthouse steps and saw him. They both froze. He took one step, and then another. Suddenly they were running toward each other and he swept her up into his arms.

She felt incredible. She smelled incredible. She was there for him after all. He hadn't been sure after everything that happened. He lifted his head to kiss her and tasted salt on her lips.

She was crying.

"Oh sweetheart don't cry. Please?"

She didn't say anything. She just nodded her beautiful head and continued the water works. Devlin put his arm around her shoulders and walked across the street to the SUV. He clapped Donnie on the back and climbed into the drivers seat.

"Where are we going?"

"They wouldn't drop the charges even though they're complete bullshit. You know that, right?"

"Yes. I went back in and told them you were with me again. They didn't listen."

"You didn't have to do that. But for now, I'm out on bail and I have to wear a monitor. They're coming to the clubhouse later to fit me with one."

She didn't say anything but Donnie leaned forward.

"It will be good to have you around all the time Dev. We missed you."

"Fill me in on what I missed when we get back. First thing I need is a shower."

"What's the second thing?"

Dev just grinned and glanced at Kaylie, leaving no doubt of what he meant. He wanted her.

"Okay man, what about the third?"

"Food. And a plan. We need to nip this shit in the bud."

"I hear that."

They pulled into the clubhouse parking lot and a stream of people poured out to greet him.

****

"You don't mind do you babe?"

Kaylie was enveloped in Dev's arms. They were finally alone in the small apartment above the club he used sometimes. It was just a bedroom with a small bathroom attached, but it was clean and had a place to sleep when he was at the club too late to go home. There were other bedrooms for rest of the Spawn throughout the clubhouse but this one was the most private and reserved for the President alone.

He was kissing her passionately for a while before he turned his head and rested his nose in her hair.

"Damn, you smell so good and I'm so filthy. I shouldn't be touching you."

"I don't mind."

She hadn't answered his first question about staying in the clubhouse. He didn't press her, thank goodness. She would have much rather visited with him at his house, or hers. It was true though that she didn't mind that he was dirty. It just felt so good to be in his arms again.

"Hmmmfff... oh god. Let me get washed up. I want to hold you."

She nodded and watched him strip down. He didn't just want to 'hold' her. That much was obvious. A thrill went through her as he exposed his body to her. He was pushing his jeans down over his washboard abs when he looked up and caught her staring. He grinned and stood proudly in front of her, his arousal already evident.

"Unless you want to join me?"

Kaylie shook her head breathlessly. She was already feeling overwhelmed and needed the time to get herself together. He sniffed himself and cringed.

"Yeah, I don't blame you. I'll be out in a flash."

Kaylie smiled as he disappeared into the bathroom. She looked around the room. He didn't keep much there. A few magazines and books. Clothes. A mini fridge. And of course, the bed… which she would be laying down on shortly. She felt butterflies fill her stomach as she looked at the bed. Would it be different this time? Now that she knew what to expect?

There was a mirror over a dresser and she walked over to it. She pulled off her sunglasses and put them aside, shaking out her hair. She stared into her eyes and tried to figure out what she was going to do… she knew what she wanted but she didn't know what she could handle… not yet.

There was only one way to find out.

Pictures were taped to the edges of the mirror. Johnny with a young Devlin and a pretty woman who must have been their mom. She traced the picture with her finger. He looked so young. But he already stood with bravado, clearly aware of his position as the man of the house. He couldn't have been older than sixteen and yet he looked utterly confident in every way. So young, but already a man. Already a protector.

It must have killed him that he couldn't save them.

She felt him behind her before she saw him. She closed her eyes as he pressed his body against her back, wrapping his arms around her waist. He kissed the crook of her neck as her head fell back onto his shoulder. Hot spirals of desire shot through her body. She knew that whatever her decision was, she would never have anything like this with anyone else.   She opened her eyes and saw him staring at her in the reflection of the mirror. He was looking at her with a fierce look in his gaze. Affection, tenderness, possessiveness and something else...

Pure heat.

Her mouth opened in response to the look in his eyes. His hand slid up her body to cup her breast as he held her facing the mirror. He played with her nipples through her dress before letting his hand drop to the hem of her dress. She started panting as he lifted his hand up under her skirt to find her panties. Without breaking eye contact, he started to tease her, stroking the line of her cleft.

She could not have pulled her eyes from his even if her life had depended on it. She gave into the delicious feelings he was creating in her as he toyed with her femininity. He was clearly not in a hurry, despite everything he'd said before. Finally he pulled her panties down and started to explore her body in earnest. He released her waist and she leaned forward slightly, gripping the edge of the dresser for support.

She moaned as she felt him lift her skirt from behind and hold the tip of his cock at her entrance. He was staring down at the place where their bodies met but he glanced up at her before he pushed forward. He was making sure she was ready, that she wanted him. He was asking permission.

Whatever he saw on her face was more than enough. He grunted as the tip of his shaft slid inside her. He held her hips with both hands as he pressed forward. Watching him take her in the mirror was intoxicating. When she looked over at herself she almost didn't recognize the wanton woman being taken from behind. And loving it.

As soon as he was fully inside her everything changed. He dipped his hips and circled them, changing the pressure and angle without withdrawing. She would have fallen over at the sensation if he hadn't gripped her shoulder with one hand. His other hand slipped down and under her skirt again, toying with her jewel.

"Ohhhhh…"

He grinned at her reflection in the mirror as he worked her body with incredible skill, taking what he wanted but giving so much more. His finger picked up speed as he ground himself deep inside her, making her clench down on him without thought.

"Unfff… oh Kaylie… yes…"

She was whimpering like an animal as he brought her closer and closer until she finally tipped over the edge. Her body shook convulsively as he pumped himself into her with greater force now. She was gripping him unconsciously when she felt his shaft jerk inside her. Then he leaned forward over her, thrusting wildly as he unleashed himself against her womb.

He didn't stop moving until they were both spent. He kissed her neck tenderly before pulling himself from her body. He bent down and slowly pulled her panties back up from her ankles, smiling wickedly at her in the mirror. She closed her eyes as he adjusted her clothing back to normal. She opened her eyes and looked at herself. You would never know the proper young woman standing there had just rutted like an animal and loved every second of it.

Dev was pulling clean clothes on. She noticed he didn't bother with undershorts again. He grinned at her and sat on the bed, patting the spot beside him. She walked over and sat down.

"Are you hungry?"

"Not really."

He put his hand on hers and she got a terrible feeling that he was about to say something she didn't want to hear.

"Kaylie..."

"Yes?"

"Did Officer Grant mess with you- or touch you in any way?"

She looked at him, taken aback by the question.

"What do you mean?"

"I won't be angry sweetheart. Did he make you do anything?"

"No."

She looked away and crossed her arms over her chest, suddenly feeling ashamed. She'd done her best to put the whole thing out of her mind, and now he wanted her to revisit it? He put his hand on her back and stroked her soothingly.

"Kaylie? You can tell me. I gotta know sweetheart."

She took a deep breath.

"He didn't touch me. He just- looked at me."

She felt Devlin tense up beside her.

"What do you mean? Tell me exactly what happened Kaylie."

"He drove me home and he kept saying things about you- about how people call you sloppy seconds sometimes and he wanted to know if I knew what that meant."

Devlin cursed under his breath.

"Kaylie-"

Once the words started she couldn't stop them from pouring out.

"He told me what it meant. He said you had a different girl every night and the rest of the club took them when you got bored with them. He said he'd wait in line for sloppy seconds like me. He told me that I was damaged goods around here now that I'd been with you but that he wouldn't mind even if other guys did. He wanted to know if I'd been passed around the club yet."

Devlin's hand stopped stroking her back as she felt him clench his hand into a fist.

"Kaylie I swear to you that this is not like that. You are not like that. Not to me, or any-"

"And then- when we finally got back to town- to my street- he pulled over and he wouldn't- he wouldn't-"

His hand was back, holding her tightly around the waist, his head leaning into hers, resting it on hers, as if he was trying to absorb her pain.

"He wouldn't unlock the door. He just- looked at me. You know. At my chest. And- lower... He just sat there licking his lips and staring at me."

"He's a dead man."

She swallowed back tears. She hadn't told her mother or anyone what Grant had done. What he had implied that he could and *would* do. Soon.

"I'm so sorry baby. I promise you that will never happen again. He's gonna pay for that. In spades."

"No- please- I don't want you to get into trouble. I want you to be safe. Please Devlin!"

She turned into his arms and stared up at him entreatingly. He was furious. His jaw was locked and the look in his eyes would have been terrifying if it hadn't been anger on her behalf. She'd never seen him like this. But she had to make him promise her. She loved him. She couldn't let him do something stupid on her behalf.

She loved him.

"Promise me Devlin!"

He took a deep breath and nodded once, sharply.

"Good. Because I couldn't stand it if anything happened to you- because of me..."

She stood up and walked out of the room. Her pace quickened in the hallway until she was on the stairs, then running through the clubhouse to the street. She was out of the gate and a block away before he caught up- banging on the fence and calling her name. But he couldn't go after her. She'd known that when she ran.

****

Devlin was beside himself. He walked behind the club and found some old plywood to break. He kicked it until it cracked in half. Then he found another piece. This time he used his fists. After about twenty minutes he looked up and realized he had an audience. About twenty bikers and chicks were standing nearby watching him. He didn't blame them for staring. He never lost control like that.

"Grant. He's done."

Jack and Donnie looked at each other. Donnie cleared his throat.

"You want me to go to Mae's tonight?"

Devlin nodded. He could feel the pulse in his cheek from clenching his jaw so hard. His knuckles were bloody and raw but he didn't care about any of that.

What the hell was he going to do?

He felt sick at the thought of Grant treating Kaylie that way. Like she was a whore instead of his sweet angel. She hadn't wanted to tell him about it. She was trying to protect him he realized. Just the way he hadn't been able to protect *her.*

He walked back into the clubhouse and poured himself a shot of tequila. The first of many to come he decided. He started slowly but worked steadily toward oblivion. He was still sober when the technicians came to outfit him with an ankle bracelet. After they left though, all bets were off. He knew that Kaylie wouldn't be back tonight. He was starting to wonder if she'd be back at all.

Devlin stared straight forward as people clapped him on the back, congratulating him for getting out, saying he'd beat the rap, not to worry. He ignored them all, just stared straight ahead and imagined tearing Grant's head from his body.

He'd do it too. It didn't matter that he'd promised Kaylie he wouldn't. He'd messed with his woman. It was a point of honor now.

And a warning to anyone who ever considered messing with her again.

As if things couldn't get any worse, Dani chose that moment to walk into the clubhouse. She looked rough. It had been dark the night of the carnival so he hadn't noticed it, but she did look like she'd been beat up.

"Um, Dev? Can I talk to you for a second?"

He gave her a hard look. He was tired of her bullshit but she did look like she had something important to say.

He nodded curtly and turned back to his drink.

"Make it fast."

She stepped closer and lowered her head.

"The night of the carnival I talked to Grant. He said he wanted to put you away. I told him I would help him."

Devlin's head shot up from the bar.

"You what?"

"I know I shouldn't have but I was so mad at you. I wouldn't have actually done anything Dev, I swear."

He narrowed his eyes and stared at her. She did look contrite.

"Go on."

"When I asked him what he meant to do he said he was going to kill two birds with one stone. The first stone was getting himself laid. The second one was-getting you put away. For good."

He stared at her realizing what she was saying.

"He hurt you?"

She nodded.

"I'm almost glad he did. Because if I had turned on the club then I would have deserved it. But I didn't go through with it. He spared me that at least."

He stared at her, cursing under his breath.

"They wanted me to press charges against you Dev but I wouldn't. I'm so fucking sorry."

He nodded again and turned back to his drink.

"You are banned from the club."

She let out a tiny sob and turned away but he stopped her.

"Oh, and Dani?"

She turned back, fear and hope in her eyes.

"I'll make him pay for what he did to you. I promise you that."

She inhaled sharply and he saw a glimpse of the pretty girl he'd known so many years ago. She nodded, proudly this time and walked out of the club with her head held high.

12

Kaylie served a cheeseburger and turkey club to Mr. and Mrs. Marcus. They were a sweet old couple who came in at least once a week. Kaylie had always imagined she'd have something like that someday- growing old together, taking walks, raising a family.

But how could she ever have any of that with Dev?

Maybe he wasn't the problem. Maybe it was her. His lifestyle was extreme to be sure but he'd shown her that he was a good man time and again. Better than most she'd wager. So what if he rode a bike and hung out with a bunch of tattoo'd tough guys. They stuck together like glue. If any of them ever needed anything, Dev would be there for them and vise versa. They had loyalty and guts in spades. *Especially* Dev.

If she couldn't get past all of this then she knew she would be the one missing out. She had no doubt that

Devlin would have another woman just by snapping his fingers. He might miss her, or even be really sad for a while, but she doubted he would experience the soul crushing loss that she was anticipating. Just thinking about being without him made her feel desolate and alone.

Maybe it was just better to turn a blind eye to the club and the troubles that went hand in hand with it. If the cops wanted to harass her, so be it. She would just toughen up. She loved Dev already. As time went on she was realizing that she wasn't even close to done falling for him. In fact, she couldn't think about anything else but him, and the way he'd made love to her that afternoon.

Her cheeks were flushed as she walked to Mae's to do her night shift. She had been glad for an excuse to get out of the club house. She'd needed time to think and she was almost certain she'd made her decision. Whether it was the right one or not was hard to say.

She tied her apron over her pink rayon uniform and got to work. It was busy tonight which was a blessing. It kept her mind off of... other things. Images of Dev and Grant were swapping places in her mind with intensely different results. She went from feeling very warm in the diner to wanting to run out back and upchuck all over her tennis shoes. So being busy was great. Until he walked in.

Officer Grant.

Her stomach felt like it dropped to her shoes. He was looking around the place as if he owned it. He caught sight of her behind the counter and his expression changed to one of unconcealed lust. He oozed his way toward the counter like the slime ball that he was and sat down in front of her.

He rested his big meaty hands on the formica counter. She had trouble looking away from them for a minute. Officer Grant was a huge man. Tall and strong but also getting close to thirty and starting to get fat. His hands looked pink and swollen laying there on the counter like two uncooked chicken cutlets. If he touched her with them she'd scream.

"Well, if it isn't my favorite little waitress. How are you doin' tonight honey?"

She flipped over her pad and stared at it, pen at the ready.

"What can I get you, Officer Grant?"

A disgusting smile crept over his face as he pondered the question. It was obvious that he was thinking about things that were *not* on the menu. And never would be!

"I don't know doll face. Do you have any specials tonight? Maybe a discount on something leftover, like sloppy seconds?"

She swallowed the bile rising in her throat. Was he kidding with that BS? Suddenly she started hoping that Dev would do something to the guy. Not kill him but... something bad.

Maybe she was cut out to be a biker's woman after all.

"Let me know when you're ready to order."

She slapped a menu down in front of him and walked away. She didn't see Donnie outside on his bike making a phone call.

****

Devlin was being held down by three guys. He'd taken the call from Donnie and ran out of the clubhouse before anyone could stop him. It was Jack who wrestled him off his bike to the pavement and then got a few other guys to help him hold Dev down.

Grant was at Mae's. Bothering Kaylie. Again.

His guts twisted at the thought of that pig talking dirty to his sweet girl. She'd lost her virginity less than a week ago and she was already dealing with this crap? It made his blood boil.

Enough so that he was ready to break the agreement of his release. If he left the clubhouse compound his ankle bracelet would go off and that would be it. Guaranteed jail time.

Then he wouldn't be able to protect Kaylie at all. Or touch her. Or...

He nodded curtly and the guys eased their weight off of him. He stood and brushed himself off then stalked back inside the club. He got up on a chair and put his boot on the bar.

"Listen up! We are having an outing. All of you are going to Mae's for banana splits."

A couple of the guys moaned amongst all the cheering.

"I'm lactose intolerant Dev!"

"Whatever- get what you want Lennie. The point is, that pig Grant is in there right now, messing with my old lady. I can't go anywhere. But you guys can."

In unison all the guys got up and ran for the door. The sound of 40 something hogs revving up and hitting the road was like music to his ears. He climbed down and reached behind the bar for a beer. Even the guy manning the bar had gone.

Grant was going to love this.

****

Mae's was full of leather. Kaylie stared around as she rushed to take everyone's orders. There were at least fifty bikers in the diner, all coming within the last few minutes. She saw Donnie and Jack had taken seats on either side of a suddenly nervous looking Grant.

She was worried about getting all the orders straight until she realized they were all getting the same thing. Banana split. Extra nuts. Well, all except for one guy who ordered sprite, mumbling under his breath 'food allergies.' She felt tears welling in her eyes. Dev couldn't have sent a clearer message to Grant. Or to her.

She was his. He would protect her.

Donnie was leaning in toward Grant and whispering something in an urgent manner. Jack said nothing as usual, but was following the conversation closely and nodding. When Kaylie brought Grant his check she looked him proudly in the face. Sloppy seconds didn't get this kind of escort home.

"Anything else Officer Grant?"

He shook his head and reached for his wallet. His hand was shaking slightly and his face was white as a sheet. Jack grabbed his hand, twisting it hard while Donnie grinned up at her and winked.

"No thank you. I'm- uh- sorry for not treating you like a lady."

She nodded at him regally.

"I accept your apology. Just see that it doesn't happen again. To any woman."

He nodded eagerly while his wrist was slowly wrenched underneath the counter.

"And tell Dev-"

She cocked an eyebrow at him.
"The charges are dropped."

With a whoosh of air he stood and dropped twenty bucks on the counter. In less than 30 seconds, he was gone.

A huge cheer went up from the crowd, bikers and staff alike. And then one of the prospects came behind the counter to help her dole out ice cream for everyone. He cleaned up afterwards too, much to Charlie's amusement. By the time they all left she had a stack of twenty dollar tips a couple of inches high.

****

He was waiting for her when she walked into the clubhouse. It was late. She'd finished her shift later than usual. There had been a lot of ice cream bowls to put away from what he'd heard. Jack had waited outside while Donnie went back to the club to pick up Dev's SUV.

There was a nervous knot in the pit of his stomach as she walked toward him through the crowd of bikers. They all smiled at her as she passed. She was one of them now. They loved her as much as he did.

Love. There it was again. No point fighting it now. He loved her, for better or worse. He was praying he wasn't about to get his heart ripped out by the woman he loved.

Finally she stood in front of him. She didn't smile or kiss him. She just raised her chin and stared him right in the eye.

"I didn't know if I wanted this kind of life."

His chest felt like it might explode but he forced his voice to remain steady.

"I understand. I won't be mad if this isn't what you want Kaylie. I could never be mad at you."

She looked down as if she were embarrassed about what she was saying. Like the words didn't come easy. He held his breath, hoping beyond hope that she wouldn't say they were through.

"I said I *didn't* know. But now I do."

When she looked up again he was shocked at the triumphant look blazing out of her eyes. It was strong and sure and confident. It was full of love. For him.

"I'm yours Devlin. For as long as you want me."

He almost laughed but he felt emotion choking his throat, making it tough to even talk. He cupped her face and stared into her eyes.

"Forever Kaylie. Is that long enough?"

She nodded as he watched tears fill her beautiful eyes. He clasped her to him harder and bent his lips to hers.

"Forever."

Still Waters

By

Joanna Blake

For M

Chapters

Janet stared at her shoes while her father droned on and on about responsibility. She did her best to tune him out completely. Until her mother took over the lecture, making sure Janet knew how *humiliated* she was to have a daughter like her. Then Janet tuned her out too. It was better this way. Just let them have their say and she could get on with her life.

Whatever that was going to turn out to be.

She bit her tongue to keep from talking back. They just didn't get her. They never had, and she doubted they ever would. Her parents were extremely well off and belonged to every club in town. They had the nicest house, the nicest cars, and until recently, the nicest little goody two shoes for a daughter.

She almost laughed but she didn't want to get them going again. She had been a goody two shoes. Until about a year ago. Then BAM. Not so much.

Janet had never been the sort of person who did well with a bunch of rules. She didn't care about what other people thought, not like her parents did. But she didn't want to argue. Not tonight. Tonight she was meeting her best friend Kaylie for the first time in six months. Since she'd left for college.

That had gone really well.

College had not been for her, to put it mildly. She hadn't enjoyed her classes, or the dorms or anything really. Well, except for one thing...

She rolled her eyes and forced herself to keep still. She was ready to bounce out of her chair with excitement. Not just because she was going to see Kaylie, but because of *where* they were meeting. They were going *there*. The SOS clubhouse.

Janet had never been inside the Spawn's headquarters. Few outsiders had. And tonight was her chance. Her best friend was dating the President of one of the most notorious MC clubs in all of California! She was bursting with anticipation. She wondered if there would be anyone there she might want to date too. Kaylie had warned her that most of the guys were pretty cavalier about women, but you never know. Besides, Janet could be cavalier too.

She'd been feeling particularly reckless since getting kicked out of college for poor grades. She'd spent a semester and a half on academic probation, struggling since almost the first week of school. She didn't really blame her parents for being mad.

But how could they understand what it was like? There was no way to explain it to them. College had changed everything for her. She had finally blossomed into a *woman*. She'd always been distracted by boys. But finally after all this time, *she* distracted *them* too.

How was she supposed to concentrate on school with so many

other things to do? She just wanted to dance and have fun. She'd gotten into the habit of hitting the night clubs almost every damn night. Of course she was flunking out!

She peeked up at her parents sour expression. It was painfully obvious that they were still disappointed that her ballet career had been cut short. It didn't seem fair. She was the one who'd worked so hard for all those years. And besides, it's not like they had been expecting her to go to med school. But she had been hoping in a vague way to become a physical therapist someday. She'd fallen in love with the profession after the injury that forced her to hang up her toe shoes for good. Her therapist Becky had been amazing and so smart. It was around that point that she'd started to fill in and finally develop- dun dun dun- boobs!

God, she loved her boobs. She loved the way they looked, the way they felt, and especially the way they seemed to open doors... get her out of speeding tickets... even get her free drinks. Lots and lots of free drinks.

She tugged her skirt down over the tiny heart tattoo on her outer thigh. It was a good thing they hadn't seen that yet. No reason to send them into the stratosphere. Especially since that wasn't the last tattoo she planned on getting...

After another twenty minutes of lecturing they finally seemed to lose steam. Janet had heard enough about responsibility and becoming a productive member of society for a lifetime. She wasn't sure how she was going to fit into this world just yet, but she was sure it wasn't going to be the way her parents were talking about.

Not even close.

****

Jack stood with Donnie, who was leaning against the bar, telling the guys a hilarious story about Dev and Kaylie. Making fun of the club President's sudden and utter devotion to a mere slip of a girl was everyone's favorite pastime. The Spawn's all adored Kaylie too so it was never mean spirited.

It was just too funny to see Devlin mooning over a woman when he'd had the chance to bed nearly every woman in two counties. Jack knew better though. As his second in command he knew that Dev had been needing something more than that. He had for a long time.

After Dev lost his family, the club was all he had. At 28, Jack was a couple of years older and had taken him under his wing. He'd never told the boy what to do, but he'd shown him by example. The kid had good instincts from the start. He was strong and smart and fearless, sure. But it was his backbone and sense of fair play that Jack had known would make him into an incredible leader one day. And he'd been right.

Donnie was mimicking Kaylie accepting a larger than life bouquet of pink roses, pretending to struggle under the weight as he simpered in a high pitched voice which sounded nothing like Kaylie to Jack. He rolled his eyes.

"And then she squeals 'Oh Dev! For me?'"

Everyone laughed except Jack. He'd been there. The bouquet had been at least twice that size.

"Speak of the Devil!"

Devlin eyed them as he came into the bar. He was wearing a clean and pressed shirt. That meant only one thing. Kaylie was coming to the clubhouse tonight. Jack sipped his ginger ale and scoped the bar out for trouble makers. There were always short fuses around to defuse in the SOS bar room. It was only an urgent matter when Dev's old lady was in the clubhouse though. Usually the Spawn let their guys work things out the old fashioned way.

But not when Kaylie was there. Dev was really strict about what was said and done around her. Some saw it as a sign of weakness, but not Jack.

He knew Dev was a lucky son of a bitch to have found somebody who deserved that level of care and protection. Someone who loved him back. If anything, Jack was jealous. Not that he'd ever expected or even wished for anything like that for himself.

Dogs like him didn't deserve love. He deserved dignity and brotherhood from the other Spawn's only through the dint of his unwavering loyalty. Other than that, he considered himself to be worthless. Well, except in a fight.

Jack stood well over six feet tall and was built light a freight train. With broad shoulders and a massive heavily muscled chest over narrow waist and hips, he was in peak physical condition. He'd lost the last of his padding in the last few years when he'd finally stopped drinking himself into oblivion every night. With his tattoos, muscular physique and streaming long dark hair, he'd earned himself a slew of embarrassing nicknames over the years. Unfortunately there was one that stuck.

The Viking.

He never responded to the joking around with more than a level stare. The joking usually stopped immediately. He didn't like to be teased, or taken less than seriously. But he put up with it, because he liked being in the thick of it with his fellow Spawn. His life had been so desolate before he'd been initiated. He'd ridden alone for years, hitting the road when he was just 15 on the back on a stolen bike. He was still isolated in a lot of ways, but at least he wasn't alone.

For the first time in his life, he knew there'd be someone to cry at his funeral.

2

Janet forced herself to relax as she followed Kaylie into the clubhouse. Years of dance training had given her a rail straight spine. Sometimes people thought she was stuck up because of it. She wasn't a snot, though she certainly wasn't a shrinking violet. She relaxed her body, letting it sway naturally, sinking into her hips when she walked.

Do not walk like a dancer!

She stared around the clubhouse as Kaylie led her to the bar room. The place was bigger than she'd thought. It was literally as if the most bad ass, honky tonk bar had been plopped down in the middle of the huge building, far from prying eyes. There was a long dark wood bar with a brass railing, fully stocked, two stripper poles on either end of the room, and chairs and tables everywhere.

And men. Lots and lots of men. They all turned to look at them when they walked in. Janet looked around and saw a few severely underdressed women here and there. She smiled to herself. Her mini skirt and tank top were practically modest. Not as modest as Kaylie's outfit, but close.

Devlin made a beeline for them, kissing Kaylie quickly before holding out his hand in greeting. God, he was cute. Janet couldn't help but be a little envious of the adoring way he was staring at her friend. There was no doubt in her mind that he loved Kaylie.

Some girls have all the luck.

He led them over to the bar and asked a few guys to vacate stools for them. She and Kaylie hopped onto the stools as a handsome guy with spiky black hair and bright blue eyes came over to take their orders.

"You must be Janet. I've heard a lot about you. I'm Donahue."

Janet blushed a little bit. What had Kaylie said about her to these guys? And why would a tough as nails biker give a shit?

It's because they cared about her, Janet realized. Kaylie was one of them now. Janet had never belonged to any group. Even as a dancer it had been a mostly solitary occupation. Her abilities had set her so far above the rest of the local talent that no one had really talked to her. Except her teacher Mrs. Lewis, who adored her. Until the accident. Now she was just plain old Janet Mahoney.

"Thanks. It's... nice to meet you too."

"What can I get you lovely ladies this evening?"

She glanced at Kaylie who smiled conspiratorially and leaned forward.

"Two sea breezes please."

Donnie rolled his eyes at the girly order, making them giggle. There were two other guys behind the bar running around and doing the grunt work but Donnie made their drinks, even adding fresh fruit. They turned around on their bar stools to include Devlin. He waved to a man across the room and he started over.

Janet's heart did a little flip flop at the sight of him. Now *there* was a biker. Tall and lean and mean looking. He had long dark hair and was dressed in leather pants and a club jacket, with a torn black t-shirt underneath. He didn't look to the left or the right as he walked toward them.

"This is Jack, my second in command. Jack, this is Janet."

Her mouth felt dry as the giant turned his attention toward her. His eyes flicked over her as if she were inconsequential. But then- there was a glimmer of something- *warm* in his gaze. He nodded at her, and then at Kaylie. And then he turned around and stalked back to the spot he'd been occupying across the room.

Janet's mouth must have been open as she stared at him. He was - Jesus - he was a little bit scary! Kaylie giggled and sipped the drink that Donnie had just placed in front of her.

"Don't mind Jack. He's not as mean as he looks."

"He isn't?"

Devlin grinned and grabbed the beer Donnie served him without asking.

"Jack's one of the best people I know. He just doesn't like to brag about it."

Janet glanced over her shoulder. She could have sworn Jack was scowling at her. But he turned his gaze so sharply that she couldn't be sure.

****

"What's he *doing* over there?"

Three drinks later, and Janet could not get the guy out of her mind. He'd been standing alone all night, surveying the room.

"He's protecting us."

"What?"

Kaylie leaned in.

"It can get kind of crazy in here. Jack's making sure nothing gets started while we are here."

"Oh."

A funny feeling was settling in the pit of her stomach. He was protecting them. She felt safe suddenly. Safer than she had in a long time.

Maybe ever.

Kaylie was giggling. She didn't drink too often. Janet was feeling a bit giddy herself.

"They call him the Viking. But don't do it! He hates it."

"Does he ever talk?"

"No. To Devlin sometimes. But I've barely heard more than three words out of him at a time."

"Is something- wrong with him?"

"No. And don't let anyone hear you say that. Devlin told me he owes Jack his life. He's done more for Devlin than anyone. Me too. He's a good guy. You don't have to be scared of him, I promise."

She was feeling something. But it wasn't fear.

The hairs rose on the back of her neck. She turned and caught him staring at her. No, not staring. His eyes were boring into her. She could feel his eyes as if he were touching her.

Intimately.

The Viking. It suited him.

She swallowed nervously and turned back toward the bar. She glanced over her shoulder and he was still watching her with a faint, superior smile. Her spine stiffed and she turned her back on him deliberately.

There was something about him that made her nervous. He was so… male. She'd never seen anyone that masculine in her life. He looked cold and hard, no matter how handsome or chiseled his face was. And that body… Jesus he *did* look like a Viking! Strong and lean and ruthless.

He made her nervous. Very, very nervous.

Kaylie was chatting about some of the people they'd gone to high school with as Janet struggled vainly to get her emotions in check. The drinks weren't helping.

Yes, she was nervous. But she was also aroused. She crossed her legs and pulled her top up in the front. When she snuck a look behind her, Jack was openly leering at her.

No, not at her. At her legs.

She felt overly warm in the bar suddenly. As if they'd turned up the heat like the sauna at the dance studio where she practiced sometimes. She licked her lips and nodded when Donnie offered her another drink. He was lording it up all night, bossing the prospects around. His merry blue eyes made her feel comfortable. Jack's black gaze did not.

Devlin slid his arm around Kaylie.

"You about ready to go?"

She nodded, a light blush tinting her cheeks. Janet looked away, not wanting to interrupt their intimate moment.

"Come on Janet, I'll drive you home."

She waved goodbye to Donnie as Dev threw a couple of twenties on the bar. She couldn't resist one more glance across the room while Kaylie pulled her jacket on and gathered her purse.

Jack was just where he'd been all night. He was staring toward them again. He could have been looking at any of them. Kaylie, Dev, even Donnie behind the bar. But she knew he wasn't.

He was looking at her.

****

Jack watched as Dev led Kaylie and her friend out of the bar. He could relax once they were out of the room. But he didn't feel like relaxing. He felt like breaking something.

He never resented anything Dev asked him to do. For some reason he'd felt jealous that he had to keep watch tonight. He would have rather been by the bar. With her.

Janet. Such an ordinary name for such a fiery little creature. The girl was stunning. Red hair, pale blue green eyes and a body that- well, it had his attention. That much was obvious.

Hot girls came and went in the club on a daily basis. But Janet wasn't just hot. She was fucking beautiful. There was something regal in her bearing too. She'd looked like a queen, perched with her long legs dangling off the bar stool. A queen who was up to no good. Slumming maybe.

He frowned. He didn't mess around with women too often. Once every couple of months he'd screw one of the hanger ons to keep his head straight. But never the same one twice. That was dangerous. He didn't want them to get attached to him. He didn't want to answer questions. He didn't want to talk or hold hands. He wanted to get laid and that was it.

Most of the girls around here understood that and were more than happy to oblige him, or any of the other Spawns. He had a feeling that a rich girl like Janet would expect more from him. And since she was friends with Dev's old lady, he'd certainly have to give more than he was used to.

He shook it off and left the bar room, climbing the stairs to his favorite perch on the roof. He could see at least two miles from up there, the distance making the industrial district where he lived look almost pretty. Nobody ever bothered him up here either. That was the best part.

He pulled a cigarette out and lit it. He rarely indulged anymore but he was feeling strange tonight. He was restless. That was all. It didn't have anything to do with that girl. And even if it did, she was way out of his reach.

3

Janet moaned, rolling over in bed. Her head hurt. Those sea breezes had punched more of a wallop than she'd imagined. She stared at the clock by her bedside table.

The minute hand clicked over to 7 AM.

What the hell was she doing up at 7 AM???

BANG BANG BANG BANG BANG BANG

Somebody was knocking on her door. No, knocking was too polite a word. They were *pounding.* Like her head.

"Oh God… Come in…"

"Janet, open the door this instance!"

She shut her eyes tightly. She must have thrown the latch last night in her inebriated state. She'd been in another world last night when she got home. Thinking about *him.*

She'd tossed and turned half the night. Feeling his eyes on her, even hours later. Did he like her? Want her? Or was he judging her and finding her lacking... She must seem like a silly girl to a man like him. Then again, he was loyal to Kaylie and they were the same age. But she was a very different person than her quiet friend.

Argh! Who knew men could be so confusing? In college it had been straightforward and obvious if a boy liked you or not. Now she was all hot and bothered by a man who may or may not despise her...

BANG BANG BANG BANG

"I'm coming! Jesus!"

She rolled to her feet and tentatively walked toward the door. She felt a bit off kilter but found her sea legs quickly. She almost giggled. Being hungover *was* a lot like being on a swaying boat.

She unlocked the door and opened it to see her mother standing in the hallway with a sour expression on her face. As usual.

"Janet, if you are going to live in this house, then I expect you to be up at 7 o'clock."

"Uh... okay mom."

"And I expect you to be a productive member of this household, if not society!"

Janet didn't say anything. She was standing there in her panties and a camisole looking at her mother's face. There was no love there. Just... regret. Her mother had never wanted children. She'd never said so but Janet had overheard her yelling at her father late one night. Everything that had gone wrong in her life was all his fault.

And Janet's. Just for existing.

"If you aren't going to work, you will be doing chores! I made a list. It's in the kitchen."

Her mother turned and abruptly walked away. Janet eyed her bed longingly then sighed and pulled on a pair of jeans and a t-shirt. She just knew her mother was going to make her life a living hell until she got a job.

But who was going to hire her? An ex dancer slash college drop out with zero experience under her belt? She considered asking Kaylie if Mae needed anyone at the diner but was almost afraid to. What if she was a terrible waitress? What she really needed was to get out of this house. She felt like she was suffocating here. Her parents didn't really care about her. They just cared what the neighbors thought.

By ten o'clock Janet had swept, mopped, vacuumed, raked and weeded under the rose bushes. Her mother had hovered over her almost constantly, riding her without mercy. Janet's resentment had grown to a boiling point around 3 pm, but since her mother had conveniently disappeared around that time, a patch of weeds had gotten the brunt of it.

Now she was just exhausted. She crawled into bed, still in her work clothes.

Her phone buzzed. It was Kaylie.

'Mall tomorrow?'

Janet grinned sleepily and quickly tapped back 'Yes! What time?'

'2 ish? We'll pick you up.'

'Perfect!'

Janet rolled onto her back. Tomorrow couldn't come soon enough.

****

Jack waited outside the south entrance of the mall, leaning on his bike. He didn't usually go to places like this. The smell of plastic and perfume made him uncomfortable, as did all the normal people. The Spawns weren't normal, they were the one percent. Above and apart from the throngs of average people. Jack did his best never to mix with the regular folks. He hardly mixed with anyone. But Dev had asked him to, and

Jack always did what Dev said.

Plus he'd get to see *her* again.

He'd nodded unenthusiastically when Dev asked him if he was free to go the mall. The freaking mall. But then Dev had mentioned that Kaylie's hot little friend Janet was going.

Hot was the wrong word. The girl was *scorching.*

He'd been thinking about her for two days now. That body, the red hair, those remarkable aqua eyes… those pouty cherry red lips that begged for his mouth and tongue. Jesus, he hadn't had this many boners since he was 15. He didn't like it. It was disconcerting for someone like him who liked to be in control. He scowled and adjusted his package in his jeans.

Down boy.

It wouldn't do to walk around the mall with a stiffy. He almost smiled. Actually, that wasn't a bad idea. What would the normals say about *that?*

Devlin's SUV turned into the parking lot and Jack stood up. Then he sat down on his bike again. What the hell was wrong with him???

Devlin parked and Jack watched as the girls climbed out. First Kaylie, her golden brown hair shining in the sun. A long pale leg stepped out of the backseat, and then another. Janet was wearing shorts today. Tight little denim shorts that hugged her hips and ass. And Jesus, what an ass.

She was leaning back into the SUV to grab something- her bag. He swallowed as her sweet little bottom was thrust even more prominently into view. Fuck, now he was really getting hard. He looked away and forced himself to think about something distasteful. His childhood. Basically any moment from the age of 3-14 would do. Before he'd been big enough to fight.

It worked. His body calmed down and he exhaled in relief. He raised his eyes again just as they came toward him.

****

Janet felt her heart leap in her chest at the sight of him. He was here. The Viking. He was looking at her with a slight scowl, as if he'd just tasted something bitter, like biting into a lemon.

Well, there goes her theory that he liked her. He certainly didn't look like he'd been thinking about her the way she'd been thinking about him for the past two days. She wished she'd known he was going to be there. She would have taken more time with her hair, her makeup, her outfit...

As they got closer she could see that he was staring at her legs again. No, higher. He was staring at her, right between her legs. He looked hungry. She almost fell over in shock.

"Hey man."

Jack nodded in greeting but he didn't move his eyes from her body. They slid up slowly, inspecting her. She felt her legs getting rubbery as his gaze flicked over her breasts and finally lifted to her face. She licked her lips nervously and his scowl increased.

What was going on with this guy?

Heat pooled in her belly. Just by looking at her he'd turned her to putty. Not that he appeared to care one way or the other. She literally could not figure out if he liked her or hated her. Or maybe it was a little bit of both. She decided that it would be better to ignore him. Completely. She tossed her hair and walked into the mall.

"Come on Kaylie. Don't forget to keep an eye out for any help wanted signs."

She could have sworn the scowl on his face got even deeper when she walked past him. She didn't even glance back to see Kaylie and the guys follow her into the mall.

****

Jack stood outside the store as Kaylie and Janet tried on clothes. He'd been inside, standing with Dev until Janet had tried on a slinky red dress that molded to her curves. He'd felt like he'd been kicked in the stomach.

She looked ridiculous- like a dancer on one of those stupid TV shows. It was way too provocative. He wanted to rip it off of her. He could picture the torn dress in his hands as she stood naked in front of him.

He'd never wanted anything so badly in his life.

Arousal had come crashing through him. He couldn't figure out why. Not only was she obviously a spoiled little headstrong brat, but the girl was going out of her way to ignore him. Unless... did that mean she liked him? Girls did stuff like that all the time from what he'd heard. He moaned. The last thing he needed was some little stuck up girl messing with his peace of mind. Best to ignore her. She'd go away eventually. They always did.

Unless one of the other guys claimed her for themselves. He frowned, not liking that idea. He did not like it at all. In fact, he hated it. But that's what would happen if she kept hanging around the club. He was sure of it. He'd already heard some of the other Spawns talking about "that hot little redhead piece." Being a friend of Dev's old lady made her off limits for the rough stuff, but plenty of guys would be happy to call her their woman.

Not Jack of course. He didn't want anything permanent. Especially not with her. But the thought of her with another man irked him for some reason. Maybe he could discourage her from coming around. That would solve the problem. If he didn't have to see it, he didn't have to deal with it.

They came out of the store, Kaylie swinging a bag in her hand. Janet's hands were empty. That meant she hadn't bought that skimpy piece of fabric they were calling a dress. Good. He didn't think he could handle seeing her walk around in it. She'd liked it though. Why hadn't the girl bought herself a dress?

That's what girls did, wasn't it?

****

Janet had been scanning the mall for help wanted signs since she walked in. It was a shame her parents had cut her off. That dress had been really cute on her.

She grinned to herself. Jack had certainly thought so.

The big man thought he was being subtle but she'd caught him staring at her almost constantly. Maybe he did like her, but he had a stomach ache? That's probably what it was. She smiled deviously as she imagined handing him a bottle of pepto bismol and a tablespoon.

"Look Jan- there's a help wanted sign!"Kaylie was pointing to one of the restaurants in the food court. Janet almost rolled her eyes. Great. It was a Hooters, one of those restaurants where the girls had to wear skimpy outfits while they waited tables. She was definitely not into doing *that*.

That's until she caught the look on Jack's face. He disapproved clearly. He probably thought a girl like her wasn't good enough to be friends with Kaylie. She squared her shoulders and smiled at her friend.

"Perfect."

Jacks scowl seemed to get even deeper if that was possible. She smiled and strode across the food court.

****

Jack stared as Janet filled out the application. She was going to get hired, that much was obvious. She looked over joyed to be put on display like a piece of meat. The girls that worked there were half-naked. He didn't think a girl like her should be working at a place like that.

She was too good for it.

Clearly though, the manager was thrilled with her. He kept touching her arm and smiling at her. But he wasn't smiling at her, he was smiling at her boobs.

Jack wanted to kill him.

"If you would just try this on in the back, I can take a picture and send it to headquarters."

Janet giggled and disappeared into the back with the uniform. Dev and Kaylie were sitting at the bar with their heads together. They were always like that, totally in tune. Jack walked over and tapped Dev on the shoulder.

"Are you sure this is a good idea?"

Dev and Kaylie both snapped their heads up and stared at him.

"What man? You mean Janet?"

"Yes. She shouldn't be working in a place like this."

Devlin looked baffled.

"Why not? The girl needs a job. Her parents are being real hard on her since she dropped out."

Kaylie lifted her shoulders in a graceful shrug.

"They don't need anyone at Mae's right now unfortunately."

Jack didn't say anything. He just walked away to stand near the door that Janet had disappeared into. They were missing the point. Janet chose that moment to walk out of the storage room in the tightest orange shorts and the smallest top Jack had ever seen. It was cropped to show her flat midriff and way too small. It hugged her gorgeous tits, pushing them up and out until they practically spilled over the top. He felt the blood rushing to his groin as hot lust sliced through him.

And anger.

The whole place was hooting and hollering like animals at the sight of her. Janet smiled and cocked her shoulder at the crowd, preening. Jack had to stop himself from throwing his jacket over her. A group of college guys at a nearby table started chanting.

"FRESH MEAT! FRESH MEAT! FRESH MEAT!"

Jack felt his blood begin to boil. Devlin was beside him in an instant.

"I see what you mean, man. Come on Janet, let's get out of here."

Kaylie scooped up Janet's clothes from the storage room and grabbed Janet's arm. She had the good sense to look a little concerned when one of the guys reached out to grab her breast. Jack shoved him backwards with one hand and then elbowed his buddy in the chin when he tried to intervene.

Without turning Jack drove his heel down into the little shit's foot and heard a snap. The guy let out a blood curdling wail. Jack ignored him and threw 20 bucks on the counter top. For the uniform.

It was over in less than a minute.

****

Janet was shaking as they practically ran out of the mall toward the parking lot. Once they were outside she wrapped her arms around her bare midriff. She hadn't been expecting *that.* They'd made her feel like a stripper. Worse, they'd made her feel like she was for sale.

Thank God she hadn't been alone...

Kaylie helped her pull her shirt over the trashy Hooter's top. She was wiping away the tears that came from nowhere when she caught Jack staring at her. She narrowed her eyes at him, not in the mood for his disapproval.

"What?"

"What do you do that for?"

"I don't know what you are talking about."

"Yes. You do."

She looked away, suddenly feeling more exposed than she had in the restaurant. The funny thing was, she did know. He wanted to know why she craved the attention. She licked her lips, unsure how to answer.

"You okay, Jan?"

Kaylie was back, putting her arm around Janet's shoulders. She nodded and stood up straight. No harm done. She would just have to find a job somewhere else.

"I'm good, thanks."

Devlin looked relieved that she wasn't going to cry anymore. She almost smiled at the way he was already treating her like an older brother.

"We better go. I need to get these two little missies home to their mamas."

Kaylie giggled at Devlin as he pulled her into his arms for a kiss.

Janet opened her mouth and said something that surprised even her.

"Jack is taking me."

Kaylie's mouth dropped open before widening into a huge grin. Devlin looked thrilled. She slid her eyes sideways, peeking at the huge man standing beside her. Jack hadn't said a word but Dev and Kaylie's big smiles had clearly irritated him. Devlin slapped him on the back. Hard.

"Alright man! Have a good night."

And then they were gone, leaving Janet standing all alone with Jack in the Mall parking lot. He shifted his eyes toward her and raised an eyebrow. She lifted her chin. She wasn't going to let him intimidate her.

"So? Are we just going to stand here all night?"

He grunted and grabbed her arm, pulling her toward his bike.

****

Jack stared straight ahead, trying to focus on the road. He'd never ridden with anyone on the back of his bike before. He could feel her slender arms wrapped around his waist with surprising strength. She had a good grip for such a tiny thing.

That's right. Kaylie had said she'd been a dancer. It made sense with the graceful way she moved with him on the bike, unconsciously leaning into the turns with him.

He'd given her his helmet and thrust her onto the seat, trying not to stare at her spread thighs beneath him. Then he'd climbed on and started the bike without hesitation. He made sure she understood that he was annoyed with her. That this ride was a one time thing.

All without saying a word.

The mall was a half an hour from town, which gave him plenty of time to enjoy her body pressed against his back. And he was enjoying it. A lot. He groaned inwardly. It was his front he'd like her pressed against. He wanted her. Badly. He might as well stop lying to himself about it. The little minx was getting to him whether he liked it or not.

Perhaps he should bed her. He'd make it clear that it was just the once. Or maybe a couple of times, all in one night. That would give him time to explore her, to take her all the different ways he wanted to... He'd taste her first. Then once she was writhing in ecstasy, he'd slide into her body and wrap those long, elegant legs around his hips. Then he'd ride her, as hard as he wanted to. He'd show her that he wasn't the sort of man to be trifled with. Afterwards he'd tell her to wait until he wanted her again. It probably wouldn't take too long, given the state she'd put him in these last couple of days.

He'd take her from behind the next time. So he could see that sweet little ass up close. He almost lost his focus on the road at the thought. His mind wandered again. Toward the end of the night he'd be gentle with her. Maybe he'd even let her be on top. She'd look good riding him. Then he'd drop her off somewhere and that would be it. She'd be out of his system.

It was an excellent idea.

It was a terrible idea.

He knew Dev wouldn't like it if he treated his old lady's best friend as a disposable lay. Hell, he wouldn't like it either. The girl deserved more than that. She was proud. He didn't want to humble her. That surprised him. He'd never thought about a woman's feelings before. Or his own.

Jack didn't allow himself to have feelings at all.

Best to leave her alone. It'd be safer for everyone. She was too delicate to handle what he wanted to dish out on her. And he didn't want to make those beautiful aqua eyes fill up with tears when he was done with her.

But when he parked in front of her house and stood up, his good intentions fled. She was staring up at him as she struggled to remove her helmet. He reached out and brushed her hands aside, easily opening the latch. Her hands stilled underneath his at the look on his face. He could tell she was feeling it too- whatever this crazy feeling was.

Before he knew it, he'd hauled her up off the bike and into his arms. He grunted as her tight little body pressed against the hard wall of his chest. Her breasts pressed into him as her eyes opened wide. His mouth was on hers before either one of them knew what was happened.

Dear God.

White hot lust pierced him as he plundered her sweet, willing mouth with his tongue. His hands were all over her, caressing, touching, feeling, until they settled on her bottom. He yanked her against his erection with tremendous force. She made a startled little sound beneath him and reality came crashing back in. He tore his mouth away from hers with a soft curse and climbed back onto his bike. He felt her hand on his shoulder but shook it off.

"Wait- your helmet."

"Keep it."

He didn't turn to look at her. He realized suddenly that he was afraid to. Afraid of what he might do.

"Jack- why are you angry at me? I- I like you."

Her soft admission sent an odd feeling to the pit of his stomach. He pushed it down as hard as he could.

"You don't want to mess with a guy like me."

"What if I do?"

"Trust me. You don't."

He drove away without a backward glance. He wouldn't see her again. If Dev asked him to escort her somewhere again, he'd explain that he didn't like the girl. That she got on his nerves with her flashy ways and girlish laughter. It was better that way. He drove away, satisfied that the matter was behind him.

There was just one thing that was bothering him.

She'd been kissing him back like she wanted him as badly as he wanted her.

****

He knew where she lived.
That was the first thought Janet had as she watched him ride away. He'd known without asking.

But what did it mean?

Janet had a sinking feeling that she was in terrible trouble. Not just her life, which was a mess and damn if that wasn't a well known fact. But now she had a strong certainty that she wasn't going to forget Jack, his eyes, or his kiss any time soon.

If ever.

He wanted her as much as she wanted him. Of that she was sure. She could feel it in the way he held her, touched her, kissed her with an urgency that had taken her breath away. And yet he was the one who'd pulled back when they both knew she wouldn't have stopped him from going further.

She would have climbed on that bike and followed him straight to hell if he'd asked her.

Maybe it was a good thing he hadn't. Maybe he was trying to protect her from him, the lifestyle, everything.

But who was going to protect her from herself and her foolish wish to be near him? She stared down at the helmet in her hands. She'd loved riding with him. His confidence on the road had been incredibly attractive. Everything about him was appealing to her. Not just his strong masculine body or soulful eyes. Not just the way he smelled like leather and smoke. Not just his long hair or bad boy tattoos. Him.

All of him.

She walked into the house and straight into her room. She kicked off her shoes and crawled into the bed, still cradling the helmet.

She was in trouble.

But what was she going to do about it?

4

Janet leaned back on the blanket and thumbed through the brochure. In the back there were a few pages that had blank spaces for her to fill out. If she had the courage to.

'Application for Physical Therapist Program'

She sighed. It was a two year program at the State School. The same one Kaylie attended. It wasn't cheap and she wouldn't qualify for student aid. Not with her grades and her parents wealth. She wasn't sure her parents were going to help her at this point however. Her mother had already hinted that they planned to cut her off. They'd never been particularly affectionate, but they had been proud of her dancing career. Before the accident. Now they didn't seem to know what to do with her.

Or even care.

Janet rolled over onto her back and smoothed down her floral sundress to cover her knees. She'd just have to get a job and go to school. Maybe she and Kaylie could get an apartment together. She needed to get out of the house, that much was for sure.

"What am I going to do Kaylie?"

Her friend sat beside her, taking notes for her history exam. She put her book down and sipped some lemonade.

"You'll figure something out Jan. I'll help you."

"Yeah… but what?"

"You'll get a job and apply to the program and then we'll see. I believe in miracles you know."

Janet rolled her eyes and turned onto her side.

"Right. Just like that."

She snapped her fingers. Kaylie giggled and squirted lemonade at her through her straw.

"Hey! And I was going to ask you to move in with me!"

Kaylie sobered quickly and looked away. Janet's eyes widened.

"What is it? You don't want to be my roommate?"

"No. It's not that. It's just that- well, Dev asked me to move in with him."

Janet squealed and threw her arms around Kaylie.

"Oh my god! That's amazing!"

"I don't know. It's kind of a big step. And then my mother would be alone."

"Maybe I can move in with her instead."

Janet flopped back onto her back and stared up at the sky. Kaylie laughed.

"Sometimes I think I'm too young but other times... I love him so much you know?"

"I can tell. He loved you too. You are really lucky."

"Come on Jan, don't tell me you didn't find someone at school. You're gorgeous! I mean you always were pretty, but now, you look like a movie star!"

Janet rolled her eyes.

"Jack doesn't think so."

"Oooooh…. I knew something was going on!"

"Unfortunately that is not the case."

"Do you like him? I could have sworn I saw some sparks flying."

"I thought I did. But he has no interest in me whatsoever."

"I wouldn't be too sure. Jack's the most loyal person I know. He hides his feelings though. Still waters run deep."

Janet just snorted. That's one way to put it. Kaylie nudged her in the shoulder.

"What happened? Tell me!"

Janet sighed. She might as well tell Kaylie. At least then she might feel like it really happened, instead of feeling like some sort of dream.

"He kissed me. And then he told me to go to hell."

Kaylie started laughing uncontrollably. Janet stared at her, annoyed.

"I'm pouring my heart out and you think that's funny?"

"I'm sorry- it's just- oh my gosh - the fact that he said anything to you is kind of amazing. He never talks. Especially not to girls!"

"Well, he didn't say much. Just told me to stay away from him."

"That's interesting. Because it doesn't look like he's staying away from you."

"What?"

Janet sat up hastily and pulled the straps of her sundress back into place. Kaylie hadn't been kidding. Devlin and Jack had just parked their bikes out front and were walking around the side of the house toward them. She closed her eyes, willing her heart to slow down. Then she laid back down on her stomach and stared blindly at the application. She picked up a pen and started filling out the paperwork. Well, she filled her name in anyway.

"Hey babe."

"Dev!"

Kaylie was on her feet and leaping into Devlin's arms. The squeals of happiness behind her made Janet cringe. She pretended to be engrossed in what she was doing. A pair of enormous boots came into view. Jack was standing beside her, looming over her.

That put all sorts of illicit thoughts into her head.

"What are you doing?"

She rolled over to her side so she could see him. She scowled. Two could play at that game.

"It's an application."

"For what?"

"School. What do you care?"

He just grunted and walked over to a lawn chair nearby. He sat down and stared at her moodily. She sighed audibly and turned back to her papers. Behind her she knew that Kaylie and Devlin were watching the exchange. She could tell from Kaylie's muffled giggles that they were finding the whole situation vastly entertaining.

"Jan, there's a party tonight at the clubhouse. Devlin said we can go!"

She rolled to a cross legged position and smiled at Dev. *He* was nice to her at least.

"I thought you didn't go to the parties, Kay."

"This is a cookout so it starts early. Things start getting a little crazy after ten or eleven."

Janet chewed her lip thoughtfully.

"I doubt my folks will let me out. It was hard enough to get them to let me out of the house in broad daylight."

She sneaked a glance at Jack who was still watching her. Frowning as usual.

"But I'll ask."

Kaylie sat back down on the blanket with her and threw her arms around her.

"Come on, it'll be fun! Dev says they make the best homemade barbecue sauce."

Kaylie's mom came out with more lemonade and a couple of beers for the guys. She seemed to like Jack almost as much as Devlin. Janet ignored them all and tried to finish filling out her application. After twenty minutes she'd only gotten through one page. She was about to give up and leave when she glanced up and saw that Jack was staring at her again.

He looked... Jesus! Damn if he didn't look like she'd hurt his feelings! He caught her looking at him and abruptly stood up. The next thing she heard was the sound of his bike tearing out.

He'd left without a word to anyone.

****

Jack was staring at the door of the clubhouse bar. He was watching to make sure Janet didn't show up and ruin his night. He really was hoping her parents had told her to stay home tonight.

God, he was such a liar.

He'd been in a tailspin all day. First he'd walked into Kaylie's yard to see Janet looking like a barefoot princess. With no makeup, and her flaming red hair loose around her shoulders, she'd looked like something out of a fairy tail. Jesus, who knew a sundress could be so arousing. He'd finally decided he was going to have to do something about this insane attraction he was having to the girl. She'd chosen that moment to be a complete brat and ignore him!

He sipped his ginger ale and stared down at it disgustedly. What he needed was a real drink. It was getting late and Dev had already left with Kaylie. Nobody needed him for anything. It had been a long time since he indulged in more than an occasional beer but he wanted to numb himself to these unwelcome feelings the girl was bringing out in him.

To hell with it.

Jack strode across the bar and put his empty glass down in front of Donnie, who was lazing around back there while the prospects did all work as usual.

"Tequila."

Donnie quirked his eyebrow at Jack but didn't hesitate to pour him a shot. He held up a cold beer chaser and Jack nodded. Donnie watched him as he downed the shot and the beer in less than a minute.

"Another?"

Jack nodded again. It was going to be a long night.

****

Janet stared at her open window. She'd been stuck in her bedroom all night. Her mother had been especially annoyed that she'd gone to Kaylie's house without asking, not caring that they'd been studying. She's sent Janet to her room immediately following dinner. *Without* her phone.

She'd read a magazine, she'd finished her application, she'd looked in the back of the supermarket circular for jobs. She'd even found a few places that might be interesting and made a neatly written list of the names and numbers. But nothing could keep her mind from wandering to Jack. She wanted to be at the club tonight. To see him and be near him. She didn't care if he didn't like her. She'd make him like her if it was the last thing she did!

She glanced at her clock. It was almost 11. Kaylie might not be at the club anymore. She shrugged and pulled on a mini skirt and halter top, dabbing some lipstick on. She yanked on a pair of old cowboy boots and quietly slid open the window. It wasn't the first time she'd snuck out of her bedroom window, and it wouldn't be the last.

Five minutes after she'd made her decision, she was running through the cool grass across her neighbors lawn to the street. Only fifteen blocks to the club. She'd be there in no time.

5

Jack was leaning against the bar considering the wisdom of another shot when he heard it.

"Hey Red!"

His head snapped up and he saw her, looking tentatively around the bar. She looked nervous. She should be. A couple of guys were already trying to offer her drinks. She was doing her best to decline them, he could see, but that wouldn't last for long.

Women did not come in here at this hour looking for a drink. Especially not looking like her. She should have known better.

Damn it.

He strode across the bar and shouldered aside two Spawns who were leaning over her. Her big aqua eyes widened as he closed his hand around her arm and pulled her with him to his spot at the bar. He lifted her up and deposited her on a stool and went back to sipping his beer. His tenth. He thought it was anyway.

Hell, he'd lost count after 7 shots and chasers.   He slid his eyes sideways and watched as Donnie brought her a sea breeze without her asking. She sipped it daintily and tried to continue ignoring him. It was impressive, considering he was standing right next to her and staring at her. He turned his body toward her and tilted his head to the side, letting his eyes wander all over her. He wanted to look at her. He was a man, she was a woman. Why should he hide it?

She finally glanced at him and tried to smile. They both knew she was attracting unwanted attention from every corner of the bar. She was hot *and* she was new. Everyone wanted a taste.

"You shouldn't be here."

"I was- looking for Kaylie. I guess she left already?"

He didn't say anything, just looked her over, considering what kind of trouble he was about to get himself into. She crossed her legs nervously, revealing a long smooth thigh.

Screw it.

Jack grinned suddenly. She caught the look on his face and blanched. She thought he was laughing at her. But really he'd just decided to stop fighting it. He was going to have her beneath him. Maybe even tonight.

She crossed her arms over her chest, accidentally pushing them closer together. He stared at the luscious mounds where they pressed against each other, creating a deep cleavage.

Definitely tonight.

He tore his eyes away from her chest and looked at her beautiful face again. She looked absolutely mortified. He could see tears welling up in her eyes.

"I think I should- go home-"

He lifted her off the bar stool and set her on the floor, inches from his body.

She looked up at him, utterly confused. He couldn't wait to take her home. He'd denied himself too long already. He took her hand and dragged her through the bar room. But not to the front.

He was taking her to the back.

****

He held out his hand for her, his eyes willing her to obey him. She was about to toss her head and ignore him, like she always did when someone told her what to do. But there was something urgent in his eyes that made her pause. Before she knew it he had somehow dragged her out of the club and into the back alley. He leaned her body against the brick wall. Then he boxed her in, standing incredibly close to her. She could feel waves of heat coming off of him as she stared up at him.

He was always so calm. But he didn't look calm now. He looked angry.

And something else... hungry. His eyes flicked to her rosebud lips and she felt her heart jump in her chest.

He wanted to kiss her. Again.

She swallowed nervously. She had been waiting for him to kiss her again all week. Would he? He hadn't been pleased to see her walk into the club tonight. Maybe if she apologized, he wouldn't be so angry with her.

"I'm sorry if I made you mad. I know now I shouldn't have come."

He just looked down at her, doing nothing. His body was so close to hers. She couldn't help it. She wanted it closer. Suddenly a smile flitted across his face. But it wasn't a friendly smile. It was menacing, like a wolf smiling at a lamb he was about to devour. He lifted his hand to her face, cupping it gently. She gasped as his thumb brushed her lips.

"No, you shouldn't have."

Then he was kissing her. There was nothing gentle about it at all. He was kissing her *hard.* She moaned and opened her mouth under the assault, allowing him in. His tongue swooped in and twirled against hers, taking her.

Claiming her.

Sweet Jesus he was a good kisser!

He kissed her endlessly, far past the brief kiss of the other night. He'd left her wanting then. But now he was holding nothing back.

Not with his mouth anyway.

His hands were balled into fists, pressed against the brick wall above her. He was restraining himself somehow. She knew it. She felt it. And then everything changed.

She moaned as one hand found her body, and then the other. He didn't hesitate now. One hand grabbed her hip, pulling her against his obvious arousal, the heat of it burning her through their clothes. The other hand slid up from her waist to her chest, kneading her breast firmly before sliding his thumb over her sensitive nipple.

She felt the world tilting as he angled her backwards against the wall. He bent briefly to pull one leg up and around his waist, opening her femininity to his pleasure. He grunted and started grinding himself into her groin, fucking her through her panties and his jeans.

Oh God!

She was mindless, circling her hips against him, not minding as he pulled her top to the side and lowered his mouth to her bare breast. His lips closed over her nipple and flicked his tongue against it repeatedly. Her hands tangled in his hair as she realized she was getting close.

Jack was going to make her come. Standing up. In an alleyway.

His hand slipped down and pulled at the edges of her panties, seeking entrance. She didn't stop him. She *couldn't* stop him. She whimpered her need as he slid one finger under the elastic, touching her soft lips.

"Hey! Jack's having a taste of that sweet red wine!"   Raucous laughter filled the air as a group of bikers spilled out into the alley way. Jack cursed under his breath and yanked her against him, shielding her from their sight. He turned his head and raked his gaze across the group. They left in a hurry, clearly afraid of the deadly looks Jack was throwing their way.

"Sorry, man."

Finally they were gone. Jack held her for one moment longer and then let go of her abruptly. He watched impassively as she pulled her clothes back into order. She was breathing heavily, still aroused. Still wanting more.

"Is there somewhere we can go?"

He shook his head, as if just waking up from a stupor.

"No."

He grabbed her arm and propelled her through the club and into the front parking lot with everyone watching. She didn't like the way he was acting. He was treating her like a bag of trash he had to take out. She found herself fighting back tears. Again.

"Mike!"

A prospect ran up to them. She knew him from High School. He had a large red scar on his jaw. That's right. They called him Whiskey Beard.

She felt Jack thrust her away from him toward Mike.

"Drive her home. Make sure she gets inside and make sure she *stays* inside."

Mike nodded and walked over to his car. He'd been behind the bar all night working so she wasn't afraid to get into the car with him. But she wanted to stay here. With Jack.

"Wait- Jack- what's wrong? Did I do something?" He stared at her so coldly that she dropped her hand from where it had grasped his jacket. But she didn't give up. She couldn't.

"When can I see you again?"

"No repeat customers."

She felt her stomach drop as she watched him grab a scantily dressed girl standing nearby and kiss her deeply. She turned away and followed Mike meekly to his car, feeling sick.

Once again, she'd ruined everything.

She just didn't know how.

6

Jack thrust the blond girl away from him as soon as he was inside the club. He stalked up to the bar and held out his hand. Without a word Donnie handed him the rest of the bottle of tequila. He pulled on it deeply, filled with self loathing.

He'd almost taken her in a God Damn alleyway! Next to the trash. He'd treated her like *trash.*

He closed his eyes, seeing her tear filled eyes as he'd thrust her toward Mike. Why should she care if a piece of garbage like him didn't want her? But she had cared. She'd cared enough to make her cry.

Damn it.

He had work to do in the morning, a lucrative custom job, but he didn't care. He didn't care about anything in that moment.

"Hey, I heard you hit that sweet piece of tail in the back! Way to go Viking!"

He spun and saw Frankie K. The red haired son of a bitch was waiting for him to high five him.

Jack's mind went blank. He saw everything that happened next through a haze of red. It was like he wasn't even there. In the back of his mind, he wished he wasn't.

Him grabbing Frankie's hand. Him crushing his hand in his fist. Him pummeling the guy into the ground until someone pulled him off of him.

Not someone. A bunch of guys. He'd find out later it'd been five guys who pulled him back.

Frankie was screaming as he held his broken hand on the ground. Donnie pulled Jack away.

"You better jam man."

Jack almost laughed. As if that piece of shit crying on the floor mattered.

As if *anything* mattered anymore.

He picked up his fallen tequila bottle and stalked out of the bar to the back stairs and up onto the roof.

****

Janet crawled back into her window, the frame biting painfully into her stomach. She didn't care though. She didn't care about anything.

As soon as her feet hit the ground the light flicked on. Her mother sat on her bed while her father stood by the doorway. They'd been waiting for her.

She wasn't even surprised. Nothing could surprise her at this point. Jack had kissed another girl in front of her. As if she meant nothing to him. As if she were replaceable.

She stared numbly at her parents as they started to yell at her. She was a disappointment. That didn't surprise her. She was punished. Not surprising either. She was going to be locked in her bedroom until further notice.   That last one she managed to respond to, rolling her eyes.

"What if I have to go to the bathroom mom?"

Her eyes widened as her mother held out a bucket.

"You're joking."

"No, I am not. This is for your own good. You will not be coming out until we can be sure you won't humiliate us again. We know where you've been going and with whom."   Janet's jaw dropped. She almost forgot about Jack for a moment. Almost.

Her mother's cheeks were red with fury. So that's what she was worried about. Her good name. Give me a break. Janet's world titled as her father shook his head sadly.

"Bikers Janet? Really?"

They stood up and walked out of the room, shutting it behind them. She heard a dead bolt slide into place.

"What if I need some water?"

"There's a bottle on your desk."

She turned to see a small bottle of water. How long would that last? How long did they plan to keep her in there???

"What if there's a fire? Or would that solve all your problems?!?"

All she heard was footsteps walking away from her. Leaving her alone.

She glanced at the window and decided to make a run for it. Just as she reached it, her father slammed it shut in her face. She pressed her palms against the glass.

"Don't do this dad! Please!"

He ignored her, nailing the window into the frame. He was shutting her in there. Permanently.

Janet sank onto the bed and wondered how she'd managed to ruin everything. She had nothing now. No school, no freedom, no Jack.

The last one burned the most. She'd felt so alive in his arms. So desired. And she'd wanted him more than she'd ever wanted any man before. Who was she kidding? She'd never kissed anyone like Jack. She doubted she ever would again.

She pressed her hand to her lips. She could still feel him touching her... she felt hot and cold all over, just thinking about it. But he'd made sure she understood she was disposable. One of many. He probably had a different girl every night. She curled into a ball as wracking sobs shook her body.

****

Kaylie stood outside Janet's front door and knocked. She hadn't heard from Jan in three days, since the night of the barbecue. She'd heard something happened after she'd left. Something between Janet and Jack.

She couldn't help it, she was worried. Janet had always been a carefree girl, stubbornly ignoring the problems she faced at home. Lord knows she had enough of those. Her wealthy parents had put so much pressure on her to succeed as a classical dancer that it had nearly destroyed her. The accident had done more than finally end her ballet career once and for all. It'd made her invisible to her parents.

Since then, Janet had been in a tailspin. Kaylie sighed and rang the buzzer. She dreaded this conversation. If Janet was hiding out because of Jack, she didn't know what to tell her. He was a complicated guy. Devlin had told her that Jack had his reasons for being so solitary, but he wouldn't tell her why. Either way, she didn't want her friend to be hurt any more than she was already.

"Yes?"

Janet's dad was at the door. He looked over his shoulder nervously.

"You shouldn't be here Kaylie."

"Who's there?"

A shrill voice came from further inside the house. Janet's mother appeared in the doorway beside her dad. She looked crazed.

"Get out of here you tramp! I know you're the one who took my daughter to that- that place!"

Kaylie stepped backwards in shock. What was wrong with them? Where was her friend?

"Where's Janet? I haven't heard from her in days."

"That's because we took away her phone! You can tell that giant who keeps driving by to stay away!"

"Giant?"

They must mean Jack. He'd been driving by Janet's house? Since when?

Kaylie wanted to get away from these horrible people as quickly as possible but she had to find out where her friend was. Thankfully Janet's mom disappeared back into the house.

"Please Mr. Mahoney. Where is she?"

He glanced over his shoulder and smiled apologetically.

"She's in her room. But she'd not coming out any time soon. Sorry Kaylie."

He closed the door in her face. Kaylie stood there wondering what the heck was going on. She knew where Janet's room was. No one could stop her from peeking in the window.

She snuck along the side of the house and stared aghast at the hastily nailed shut window frame. They were treating Jan like a criminal. Kaylie shuddered. She might have lost her dad early on, but he'd loved and protected her. So had her mom.

Growing up she'd thought her well off friend had the best life. The big house, two parents... belatedly Kaylie realized how wrong she had been all those years.

She knocked tentatively on the window. She tried to see into the room but it was hard without any lights on inside. Janet's face appeared in the window. There were circles under her pretty blue eyes.

She looked awful.

Janet held a finger to her lips signaling silence. Kaylie nodded and waited while Jan disappeared from the window. She was back after a few moments, holding up a piece of paper with hastily scribbled words.

'Three days. No food or water.'

Kaylie covered her mouth with her hand, horrified. Janet's head disappeared from sight for a moment. She reappeared in the window with a fresh piece of paper.

'I need to get out of here.'

Kaylie nodded and mouthed 'I'll be back later! Let me talk to Dev.'

She wasn't sure if her friend understood her. She ran across the lawn, pulling her cell phone from her pocket. Dev would help her figure out what to do.

****

Janet closed her eyes and tensed her body, ready to leap out of the way. She was holding her desk chair in the air, barely able to keep it up with her trembling arms. She was so weak from lack of food but she could do this.

She *had* to do this.

Her parents had left her in there for almost four days now. Four days without food or water. Janet was starting to think they weren't ever going to let her out. Tears stung her eyes. She'd always known her mother didn't really love her, but to do this to her? And her father, weak as he was, he'd cared a little bit. She'd thought he had anyway. Apparently she'd been wrong.

Just like she'd been wrong about Jack.

She'd thought he cared about her. More than just wanting to take her to bed. He'd acted so protective of her when those guys had stepped to her at the mall. But he'd just been doing what he did. He was like a medieval knight in that way. A hero who always did the right thing. It didn't mean he cared.

Nobody cared about her.

She swallowed back the sob that caught in her throat. No time for tears. She was on her own now, once and for all. She had to do this herself. She was strong. She's survived shin splints and bloody toes on a weekly basis when she was dancing. She'd survived the loss of her chance to be a prima ballerina... the one thing she loved doing most in the world, the thing that defined her. She'd taken on of one the Spawn's toe to toe for God's sake.

She could do this.

She knew Kaylie would try to help her but she didn't know how or when. No, Janet was on her own in this. What could Kaylie do anyway? She was no match for Janet's evil witch of a mother. She said a little prayer of thanks to God for giving her one true friend.

Her only friend in the world.

Then she swung the chair back
over her head and threw it at the window.

****

Jack woke up on the roof with the
worst hangover he'd had in his life. No,
wait, that was yesterday. Or the day
before. Today was the worst hangover
anyone had had, *ever.* In the God Damn
history of man kind. He moaned and
rolled over to a seated position. It was
the fourth day of his bender.

He picked up the empty tequila
bottle and grimaced. He needed a cup of
coffee. He needed a *shower.*

"Jack man, you up there? Come
down! We gotta talk to you."

Dev was calling him. He stood
unsteadily and headed to the roof hatch.

When he got downstairs, a terrible
feeling of foreboding came over him.

Something was wrong. Something

was very, very wrong.

Kaylie and Dev stood in the back alley. She looked distraught. Hell, even Dev looked worried about something.

"Man, you look like shit."

Jack ignored him.

"What is it?"

Kaylie stepped forward nervously, as if she weren't sure she should be telling him something. He waited, watching her decide what to say. She swallowed and finally opened her mouth.

"It's Janet."

He said nothing, fully expecting her to tear into him for what had happened in the alley. What had almost happened. He almost laughed. He should have just taken her up against the wall. Then maybe she'd be out of his system by now.

God knows the booze hadn't blotted her from his mind.

"I don't know if there's anything going on with the two of you, or if you care about her but..."

He looked at Dev over her shoulder to see if his friend was mad at him. How was he supposed to explain *this* fiasco to him? To anyone?

"There isn't."

Kaylie stared at him.

"There isn't anything going on."

"Okay. I just thought maybe you wanted to help her. After what happened at the mall. I know she likes you Jack."

She did, did she? That was interesting. So they weren't there to yell at him after all.

He stared at Kaylie with one eyebrow raised. Even that movement was painful in his recently inebriated state. Kaylie let out a deep breath.

"I'm scared for her."

"What?"

He was prepared for her to tell him that Janet had gotten herself into trouble. Fine. He'd help her. He was prepared for her to tell him that Janet was angry at him and wouldn't come to the clubhouse. Even better. He was not prepared for what Kaylie said next.

Not at all.

"Her parents found out she's been hanging around the clubhouse. They-"

"They what?"

"They locked her in her room with no food or water. It's been three days at least-"

"WHAT?"

"She hasn't had any food or water in days. I don't even know if they care if she lives or dies at this point. I was going to call the police but Dev said-"

He closed his eyes and felt the deepest rage he'd ever felt in his life. Then he climbed onto his bike, and rode.

7

Jack broke about fifty laws in the fifteen block ride to Janet's house. He was angrier than he'd ever been in his life. And that was saying something.

He was off his bike and at the front door less than five minutes after Kaylie had told him what was happening. He banged his fist on the front door until a man in his early 50's opened it. He looked terrified when he saw Jack looming in the doorway.

"Where's Janet?"

"She's gone."

A pinched face woman appeared behind him.

"You're one of the biker scum that she's been hanging around with. Get out of here before I call the police!"

A voice inside Jack screamed 'I'M NOT SCUM!' with tremendous force. God, he wanted to wring their necks. How could they be so stupid?

How could they not take care of something so beautiful and precious?

And fragile.

Janet had convinced him she was tough, along with the rest of the world. But it wasn't true. She was strong in her way, that was true. She'd had to be. But there was a vulnerability about her he'd sensed and chosen to ignore. Now that he'd met her parents he had no doubt where that came from.

They'd mistreated her. Endangered her. Ignored her cries for help. He felt sick to his stomach imagining her in her room, hungry and thirsty and alone.

No. That was wrong.

He was the one who left her alone when every fiber of his being had been telling him to take care of her, nurture her, protect her.

Love her.

He did something he rarely did. Something he rarely *had* to do. He made himself look deliberately intimidating, leaning forward to sneer at Mr. Mahoney.

"Where is she?"

Janet's mother stepped forward. She looked like his beautiful Janet, but distorted in a fun house mirror. She must have been gorgeous once. Before bitterness twisted her features. No wonder Janet's dad was so whipped.

"She ran away. Maybe if we're lucky she'll never come back."

He pushed her out of the way and stalked into the house.

"Show me her room."

Her father eyed him warily and wisely decided to humor him. He led him down the hallway to a door with a massive deadbolt on the outside. Jack was horrified when he saw the size of that deadbolt. Janet was a girl, not a horse or a criminal. She hadn't stood a chance.

He stepped inside the room and winced. It smelled horrible in here. He saw a bucket full of piss and shit in the corner. He closed his eyes. They'd left her alone with a bucket.

This was his fault. All his fault. He's the one they didn't want her hanging around with. He should have left her alone to begin with. Or taken care of her. Not this bullshit waffling he'd been doing. Fighting himself every step of the way.

Now she was the one paying the price.

It wasn't right.

"Get out."

Her father was lifting the bucket when Jack snapped the order at him. He hesitated then awkwardly carried the offending container out of the room. Jack blew air out through his nose and looked around the room. He could hear them arguing out there. The woman wanted to call the police but the man was trying to convince her not to.

No wonder she'd created her own world in here. The room looked like a sanctuary. Posters of far away places covered the walls, all interspersed with stunning photos of dancers. Slender girls with long legs and frilly costumes. None of them held a candle to her.

A fabric scarf covered her lamp, lending the room an ethereal glow. He turned and saw her bed. It was a mess, with blankets and sheets everywhere. As if she'd tossed and turned on it. All alone.

Except for his helmet.

He moaned, realizing she'd been sleeping with it. He closed his eyes again, feeling a sharp sting of regret. He regretted everything he'd done since he met her.

Except kissing her. He could never regret that.

He stared at the window. She'd smashed it open after three and a half days trapped in this airless room with no food or water. Or comfort. While he'd been drinking himself into oblivion, she'd been in here, alone and afraid. Sharp pieces of glass stuck out in every direction. It was a miracle that she hadn't cut herself.

Maybe she had. Maybe she was bleeding to death in an alley somewhere.

If she died, he'd never get to tell her he was sorry.

He'd never get to tell her he cared.

He had to find her. Now. But how? She could be anywhere. Kaylie was her best friend and even she had no idea where Janet had gone. It's not like she had anyone else.

If he'd played his cards differently, she would have come to him for help... instead she was out there, in God only knows what kind of danger. He spun in a circle, scanning the room for a sign. There was nothing. If she'd taken anything with her it couldn't have been much.

Then he saw it. On the floor next to her desk was a piece of paper. He picked it up.

It was a list of names and numbers. He frowned and then realized they were jobs she meant to apply to. He read it quickly and sucked in his breath. The third item on the list was a body work place. She'd probably thought it was a place to learn physical therapy.

But she was wrong.

It was an outpost of a massive underground prostitution ring. If they got their hands on her... they'd never let her leave. He crumpled the paper in his fist and left, fear making his heart pound furiously in his chest.

8

Janet was curled into a ball on the floor, trying to protect her body in case they touched her again. She waited ten minutes in that position, making sure they were gone for real. They'd left her with a bowl of something to eat and some water and then shut off the light, leaving her in pitch darkness. She'd decided early that it was better to appear meek and afraid. So far it was working.

She was afraid, that part was not an act. But meek? Hardly.

She used her hands to feel along the concrete floor. There was no way in hell she was going to eat the food they'd left but she needed the water. She was parched. She could tell she was dangerously dehydrated. Unfortunately, that was the least of her worries.

It had been the third place she went to looking for work. The first place that hadn't cared that she'd lost her ID and didn't have references. But the joke was on her. If only there were anything funny about it.

The ad she'd found for body work had been a scam. They were running a brothel here, and from what she could tell at least 75% of the girls were unwilling participants in the scheme. Their accents told her they were from all over the world. Their eyes told her they were beaten and broken. Like her, they were the disenfranchised. No one would come looking for them.

When she'd walked in the place they'd taken one look at her and seen a gold mine. They'd told her to strip and put on some sleazy lingerie. She'd fought them tooth and nail but in the end they'd won, holding a cloth over her mouth until she stopped struggling. When she came to she was dressed in a black satin corset with lace panties, thigh high stockings and black heels.

Leaving her the heels was an oversight on their part. If anyone tried to touch her, she was going to stab them with those 4 inch stilettos. She would have already but she'd eaten the food they'd brought the first time. It was risky but she'd been so hungry at that point she hadn't cared.

Mistake. Big mistake.

It had been drugged, sending her into a stupor yet again. She'd spent half the day in a dream state, with images from her past and present intertwining. When she woke up her purse was missing. Not that she had anything in it. Her parents had taken her phone and her wallet.

She knew she couldn't blame them for this mess though. This was all her. Stupid and impulsive as usual. And now look at the situation she was in.

She wiped tears off her cheeks. At least they hadn't tried to turn her out yet. Soon though. She knew it was coming soon. She'd overheard them saying something about breaking her in before shipping her overseas.

She knew if that happened she'd disappear forever. She'd never see Kaylie again.

Or Jack.

Even if he didn't want her, she'd still like to see him now and then. Even if they didn't speak. Just his presence made her feel safe. Just his *existence.*

She conjured up an image of him. She'd been doing this for almost a week now, ever since she'd been locked in her room and then this hole. It gave her plenty of time to think… to fantasize. Mostly about Jack. As usual, he was staring at her disapprovingly. He'd be the first one to tell her she was an idiot for getting herself in this situation. Of course, he wouldn't actually say it. He'd just project it with those steely eyes of his. And then he'd smile the teeniest bit, letting her know he was glad she was okay.

Janet moved back into the corner and held a shoe in each hand.

She knew what Jack would expect her to do.

She was going to fight.

****

Jack didn't even bother with the first two names on the list. It was getting to be late at night already and he knew the legitimate businesses would be closed. But not the Body Work Special.

Christ, if she was in there, God knew what they'd done to her.

He would kill them if they hurt her. He'd kill them if they even touched her.

He texted Dev on the way. He told him to bring some guys in as few words as possible. He might need the backup. He didn't care if he made it out of there alive, but if anything happened to Janet, he'd loose his mind. Maybe permanently.

This was going to take some finessing. The Rub N' Tug was run by a rival gang. Nowhere as big as the SOS but twice as mean.

The Viper's Disciples.

He couldn't wait for the guys. If there was a chance he could stop them before they... he gritted his teeth, trying not to imagine Janet lying helpless underneath a paying customer.

He pushed open the glass door and walked in.

****

THUNK

Janet's eyes fluttered open, only to close again. Was someone here? No... she'd dropped her shoe.

Her weapon.

She struggled to wake up as the realization sunk in: they'd must have drugged the water too. She felt as if she were moving through molasses as she reached for her stiletto heel. She nearly tipped over but after three tries she had it firmly gripped in her palm.

There was something happening out side the dark room, the cage that had become her world. Loud voices, a gunshot, screams. Through her haze she merely acknowledged that there was a new development.

She forced her wayward mind to focus briefly. Maybe... maybe she could use the diversion to escape.

The darkest part of her asked where she would go... there wasn't anyone who wanted her around. Kaylie was a friend but she still lived at home. Janet tried to think of a place to run to. The only place she could think of was the clubhouse.

That's where Jack would be. Maybe he would know a place. If he could pull himself off of the sleazy blond he'd been with.

The fury that thought engendered snapped her out of her stupor. She still felt slow, she still felt weak, but she was fighting it.

And she was winning.

****

Jack stared into the terrified eyes of the woman at the front desk. She looked like an aging stripper. He didn't respond to her chirpy greeting and offer for him to peruse the menu of options. He simply said one word. Well, two.

"redhead."

The woman blanched and reached for a hidden button. Jack was on her in a second, lifting her in the air by her neck. He'd never hurt a woman, but right now he wanted to tear this bitch's head off.

"WHERE. IS. THE. REDHEAD."

The woman's eyes darted to the hallway behind him. He lowered her and released her throat just enough to allow her to gasp in some air.

"She's- in- the- back. Down the stairs and to the left."

He cursed. The basement. It sounded like a death trap. Once he got her, how the hell was he supposed to get her back out?

"What you need bro?"

He turned to see Dev and eight of the Spawn's behind him. He almost smiled at them, he was so God Damned relieved to see them.

"They have Janet. She's in the basement. Make sure everyone stays quiet."

Dev nodded and gestured to Mike, the prospect. He stepped forward and started tying up the hostess. Jack sneered at her as he passed. What kind of woman did this to her own kind?

She was a fucking cannibal.

He stormed down the hallway, leaving it to Dev and the other Spawn's to watch his back. He didn't care one way or the other. He just had to find her.

He pushed open door after door until he came to the stairwell at the end of the hallway. He couldn't hold it back any longer. He screamed.

"JANET!!!"

Everybody stopped at the guttural bellow that emanated from his gut. For a long moment everything seemed to be frozen in time while they all waited expectantly to hear her reply. It was completely silent in the low lit hallway.

Until the world exploded.

Vipers seemed to be coming out of the walls. They had guns. They had knives. They had fists.

But they never got the chance to use them.

The Viking was in full effect.

****

Janet heard the commotion upstairs. She forced herself into a state of readiness. Or almost readiness.

However ready you could be when someone had slipped you a mickey.

She swayed on her haunches, clutching a shoe in each fist. She wasn't going down without a fight. Her eyes closed sleepily and she forced them open again.

Footsteps. Heavy, loud. Running down the stairs. Toward her.

She lifted her body, ready to spring.

The doorknob turned without opening. Someone cursed outside the door. Then it was quiet.

"Get back!"

Was someone telling her to get back? She almost giggled. That didn't make a lot of sense.

BAM

BAM

BAM

The door burst inward with tremendous force, shattering the lock. Splintered wood flew everywhere but Janet didn't notice. She only knew that they'd come for her. It was time. She leapt onto the intruders back and started slamming her heel into his shoulders.

Except she couldn't seem to stab him with it. The heels kept sliding off the leather.

The leather jacket.

The motorcycle jacket.

"Jesus woman!"

She slid off him onto rubbery legs. The world started spinning as he turned to look at her.   "Janet baby? Are you alright?"

It was Jack.

She wasn't sure if she was dreaming or not but either way she was extremely glad to see him. She smiled at him wobbly as she slid to the floor.

"Hi Jack."

He cursed and lifted her up.

"Are you on something Jan?"

"Oh yes. Lots of things. Water."

She was babbling as he carried her out of the place. She saw familiar faces in the periphery. There were Spawns everywhere. But none of her attackers.

She let her head fall back onto his shoulder.

"Did they hurt you?"

"No. But if they tried I was going to stab them with my shoe."

He glanced down at her, clearly remembering that she'd attacked with the same shoe.

"Yeah, I noticed that."

She giggled at the disgruntled expression on his face.

"I still want to stab them for making me wear this trashy lingerie."

She closed her eyes and dozed off. But not before she caught the startled expression on his face as he finally took in what she was wearing.

9

Out. They were out. She was okay. Hell, she was better than okay. They must have given her some sort of happy pill. She sure did look glad to see him though.

He raised an eyebrow as he stared down at her body in that get up.

Trashy maybe. Hot? Definitely.

He realized they had an audience and he hastily tried to cover her up with his jacket. He had to put her down to get it off though. So far, she wasn't cooperating with his plan.

"Can you stand?"

She opened one eye and looked at him.

"No."

She closed her eye again, snuggling into his chest. Perfect.

Dev came over and slapped his shoulder.

"We better get out of here man. She okay?"

Jack nodded and wondered how the hell he was going to get her out of here. Then in a flash of pure brilliance he figured it out.

"Dev, I need the cabin."

Devlin looked surprised but he answered without hesitation.

"No problem, man. It's yours."

"And your car."

Dev cocked an eyebrow and him.

"Can't ride with her in this state."

Dev grinned and chucked him the keys. Jack managed to catch them without dropping Janet.

"Actually, could you open the door for me? I kind of have my hands full."

He gestured to the passed out woman in his arms. Devlin grinned and took the keys back, opening the passenger side door. Jack carefully placed Janet in the seat and strapped her in.

He turned to see 8 different Spawn's staring at him with identical expressions of shock. He frowned at them fiercely and they all scattered, hoping on their bikes.

But he wasn't really mad. He was elated.

She was okay.

They hadn't hurt her.

She was safe.

Devlin smiled and shook his head, climbing onto Jack's bike.

"Always wanted to ride this thing man. Have fun at the cabin."

****

Janet's eyes fluttered open. She was in an unfamiliar place. Not the basement anymore.

Where?

Sunlight came streaming in through a window. She could see tall trees outside and hear the tinkling chorus of song birds.

Birds?

Where the hell was she???

She sat up and swung her legs over the edge of the bed. She stood up gingerly, feeling incredibly stiff. That's when the smell hit her.

Pancakes.

There was a dresser with a mirror across the room. She hurried over to it and stared in shock at the wan looking young woman staring back at her. She was wearing a large black t-shirt and nothing else.

Not large. Humongous. It hung down to her knees.

Was she dreaming when she'd imagined Jack and the Spawn's? Was she still kidnapped?

Who had changed her out of that hooker outfit she'd been wearing?

Her stomach gurgled and she tentatively peeked into the hallway. Might as well get this over with. If she'd been sold off, she'd have to confront her keeper sooner or later.

But first she wanted to eat. She wanted to eat a *horse.*

Well, one made out of tofu anyway.

She tiptoed through the house- it looked like more of a cabin actually- following her nose down the stairs toward the delicious smells in the kitchen.

There was an old 1950's mint green table and chairs in there. A huge stack of pancakes was on a plate in the center of the tabs, along with a plate of bacon, a bowl of fruit and a carton of OJ, two glasses, and two plates. One of the plates had been eaten on. And there was an empty coffee cup.

Oh dear god, she smelled fresh coffee.

She'd never smelled anything so good in her life.

She caught movement out of the corner of her eye and turned abruptly. Someone was coming in from the deck. Leaning on the door jamb and staring at her.

Jack.

He didn't say anything at first. He just took a sip of his coffee. He looked like he'd just taken a shower. His shirt was open in the front and she could see... oh god. She could see his chest and stomach. She tore her eyes away from all that glorious man flesh to see the glint of humor in his eyes.

"Sit."

She sat. She sat down so fast that her teeth knocked together. He strolled over leisurely and picked up her plate. He piled on pancakes first, then turned to look at her.

"How long was I out?"

"Fifteen hours give or take. You're a vegetarian right?"

She nodded mutely.

"So, no bacon."

He loaded her plate with fruit and set it down in front of her.

"Eat."

She just stared at him.

"You- did all this?"

He gave her a mildly exasperated look and poured syrup onto her steaming stack of pancakes.

"Eat Janet."

She did. She put the first bite of pancake into her mouth and moaned in ecstasy. She hadn't had real food in- oh god, almost a week. She shoveled in a few more bites, stealing glances at the man who sat across from her, calming sipping his coffee.

Then she noticed something.

He had a dishtowel thrown over his shoulder.

Jack, The Viking, had a God Damn dishtowel thrown over his shoulder like a regular chef!

"How did you learn to cook?"

He stood up and grabbed the empty coffee cup, walking to the counter.

"Coffee?"

"Yes please."

He poured them each a cup from the ancient percolator. It smelled so good. He carried it back over to her and set it down. She grabbed it and inhaled deeply. She'd never smelled anything so good in her life. She'd never tasted anything so good in her life. She looked up at him, realizing he'd saved her after all.

She'd never seen anything so good in her life.

He looked so clean and good and strong. His long wet hair falling to his shoulders in waves. His tight jeans hugging that insanely beautiful body. His dark eyes watching her watch him.

That's when it hit her.

She was in love with him.

Oh dear God, she was in love with The Viking.

She would have run out of the room if she'd had the strength. This was not good. Not good at all. How could she fall in love with someone who wanted nothing to do with her?

She was an idiot, that's how.

She felt tears sting her eyes and bent forward, focusing on her food. She ate in silence for a few minutes, wishing the floor would open a large hole and swallow her up.

"Foster care."

She glanced up at him sharply.

"What?"

"You asked how I learned to cook. When I was six years old I got moved out of the orphanage into foster care."

Her mouth almost dropped open. Jack was talking to her. Jack was talking about *himself.*

"Mrs. McNealy. She was my first foster mother. I never understood why they called it that though."

Her stupor vanished suddenly. She tried to imagine Jack as a boy but it was impossible. He was so strong and tough.

"She started training me on the first day. There were a couple other kids there. We each had a duty. The girl who'd done the cooking had just left for another foster home so Mrs. McNealy decided to teach me."

"She- made you cook for her?"

He nodded.

"For all of them. Well, whatever scraps she decided to feed her wards on any given day. She might have been a mean old drunk but she liked a clean house."

"Oh god, Jack... I didn't realize you were an orphan. How long were you with her?"

He shrugged.

"A couple of years. Until the next foster house. And the next one. In retrospect, Mrs. McNealy wasn't so bad."

She took a deep breath, realizing what he was saying.

They'd hurt him.

She wanted to kill them for that. She snuck a glance at him. He was looking out the window. She realized he was letting her in, telling her something no one knew.

"You got away though."

He nodded.

"When I was 14. I'd been tinkering with stuff for years. Garbage I'd find lying around. You have no idea how much junk poor people keep in their back yards. It's like they are afraid to throw anything away. I'd found an ancient broken down Indian bike and been slowly fixing it when Norm wasn't around to stop me. He was a real cold bastard. He killed a kid once. In front of me. Made me lie to the social worked and say it was an accident."

"What would he do if you didn't?"

He rolled his shoulder and turned slightly, letting his shirt slide off enough so she could see part of his back.

She gasped.

He was covered in a blanket of scars. Huge welts. Thick ugly lines that reminded her of something.

A belt buckle. She felt her insides twist into a knot.

"As soon as that bike turned over the first I left, and I never looked back. I couldn't help the other kids. I couldn't do anything but run."

She stared at the beautiful man sitting in front of her as he pulled his shirt back on. He went back to looking out the window.

"You helped me."

He grunted and stood.

"Are you finished eating? I want to show you something."

He walked out of the kitchen door without waiting for an answer. Janet stood up and followed him onto the deck.

The house sat above a small mountain lake. There weren't any other houses out here. They were alone.

It was beautiful.

She felt Jack's hands on her shoulders and stared up at him as he slowly turned her around to face him. He was staring at her lips. He was going to kiss her!

He leaned down and whispered into her ear.

"Are you sure you're okay?"

She nodded.

He put his arms around her and smiled sweetly.

"Good."

And then he chucked her into the lake.

****

Jack watched as Janet came up sputtering. He was ready to jump in at a moments notice if she needed help of course but she looked fine.

Pissed off, but fine.

"What the hell ,Jack!"

He shrugged, liking the way the wet t-shirt clung to her curves. Hmmm... he'd have to get her out of that soon.

Very soon.

"Sorry. You smelled."

Her mouth opened and shut like a fish. He sure did get a kick out of shocking her. He grinned and started taking his clothes off. She shut her mouth abruptly and looked at him with a very different look on her face.

A very *warm* look.

He grinned and shimmied his jeans down over his hips, kicking off his boots with them. She was trying to look anywhere but at him. He glanced down and saw his cock was already rising.

And he hadn't even touched her.

He took a running leap into the water five feet from Janet. Just close enough to splash her.

He came up to catch her reaction but she was gone.

SPLASH

Water came flying at his head. She'd swum around him somehow and was pushing water at him with her forearms. Damn, she was really getting some good waves with that technique.

He was on her in an instant, grabbing her arms and holding them in the air while they both kicked their legs to stay afloat.

"Don't start something you can't finish."

She was laughing until she finally caught the look in his eyes. He stared down at this beautiful girl and watched as her eyes changed from laughter to desire. Just like his were doing.

For some mysterious reason she wanted him as badly as he wanted her. It probably wouldn't last. She was a rich girl after all. A good girl. Well, mostly. But he didn't care. If he could only have her for a little while, that would have to do.

He knew he'd want her forever.

He moaned and pulled her against him, crashing his lips into hers. He released her arms and held her head, angling it so he could kiss her deeper, harder. She made a sexy little sound of surrender as he plundered her mouth with everything he'd been holding back.

Then they started sinking.

She was laughing when she came up but he didn't smile. He couldn't. All he could do was feel and want. He propelled her backward through the water until her back was against the corner of the dock. He used one hand to hold her hips against his, pulling one leg up and around his waist.

"Unfff..."

He held them up with one hand on the edge of the dock and began again. He kissed her endlessly, nibbling her lips in between long bouts of deeply tonguing her sweet mouth. He finally lifted his head and pulled at her wet t-shirt.

"Take this off."

She shook her head.

"What if someone sees me?"

"/want to see you."

She ducked out from under his arms and swam toward the ladder.

"Come back here. Now."

He hardly recognized his own voice. He was practically growling at her. She shook her head and clambered up the ladder to the deck. He hoisted himself onto the dock and stood at the end, ten feet away from her.

Her eyes were wide as she stared between his legs at his cock. He was fully erect now and standing proud at nine thick inches. She didn't look scared though. She looked... intrigued. He raised an eyebrow at her as she backed away from him playfully.

"That's my t-shirt and I want it back."

She smiled suddenly and ran toward the house.

"Then come and get it!"

****

Janet ran up the stairs and into the bedroom she'd woken up in. She heard him behind her, his wet feet slapping the stairs. Two at a time.

He was right behind her.

She climbed onto the bed and pulled the t-shirt off. As soon as he appeared in the doorway she chucked it at him. It hit him in the face. She stifled a giggle. Her aim was better than she thought.

He pulled it his face off and chucked it aside, staring at her naked body. Then he was on the bed. Then he was on top of her.

It happened so fast that she would have missed it if she blinked.

She moaned at the incredible feeling of his hot chest pressing into her breasts. He felt so strong and hard against her softness. Then he was kissing her again. But there was more than just passion in the kiss. He was kissing her like he cared. As if it meant something.

His hands found her breasts and he lowered her head to them.

"Oh God, Janet."

She gasped as arousal shot straight to her center, spreading out in every direction. He readjusted himself so he could rub his shaft against her apex. She moaned as he stimulated her there with his slowly rocking hips without inserting himself inside her. Clearly he was not in a hurry.

She whimpered as he pulled her nipple into his mouth, tugging sharply.

Her hips were moving of their own volition. She wanted him to hurry up. She wanted him inside her now.

Right now.

He chuckled low in his throat and moved down her body. Her fingers were in his hair. Oh god- he was going to-

His lips pressed against her soft nether lips, kissing her softly. Then he pulled back and his tongue snaked out. Her whole body arched off the bed as he lapped up and down her slit, never pressing inside. He used one hand to hold her hips immobile and the other one moved above his mouth to find the sensitive nub. He started lightly circling his finger on her clit and she bucked against him.

"Jack!"

She felt him smiling as he continued his slow exploration of her body. Finally he picked up his pace as he worked her clit and slid his tongue inside her. They both moaned.

Then he started to fuck her with his tongue.

"Oh Jesus!"

She was beside herself. It was so intimate what he was doing. Never mind *how* he was doing it. He was licking her as if it was his mission in life to slowly drive her insane. It was working. She'd been shocked at first but now- now she was too desperate to be embarrassed.

She was close. He seemed to know it too. But he didn't let her go over the edge. He just kept her there, aching for him.

She was gasping for air as he lifted his head slightly to look at her. Her eyes were half open, watching as Jack devoured her sex. He lowered his head again. This time she felt his tongue on her clit as he slid one finger inside her.

"Hmmmm..."

He was really enjoying this, a voice said in the back of her head. She tried to move her hips, to pull him deeper, make him move faster, but he just laughed again and pulled her clit into his mouth, flicking his tongue against it rapidly.

"Oh!"

He was murmuring something but she couldn't understand him. He slid a second finger inside her and she moaned. She wanted- she wanted-

She screamed as the climax hit her. Her body shuddered violently as the biggest orgasm she'd had in her life tore through her body. He didn't stop the staccato motion of his tongue. He didn't stop sliding his fingers in and out of her. He didn't stop-

"Ahhh!"

She was shaking as he finally lifted his head. What he'd just done to her was like nothing she'd ever experienced in her life. She expected him to look smug but instead he looked desperate with need. He slid his body up against her until he reached her mouth. He kissed her softly, as she stared up at him. He looked like he was in pain.

"Janet... I want to..."

"Yes. Oh god, yes."

Relief flooded his features as she felt him position his shaft at her juncture. He felt hot and hard against her, like silk and steel. He braced himself above and stared into her eyes as he pushed forward.

****

Jack grunted like an animal as her warm heat enveloped him. She was so tight… and wet… and she'd tasted so God Damn sweet in his mouth. The taste of her had inflamed him to the point that it physically hurt to not be inside her. But he had to make sure she was ready.

He had to make sure she wanted him as badly as he wanted her.

He held her gorgeous hip with one hand and started to make tiny thrusts. He knew he was larger than average. Never mind that he'd never been with a woman as small as Janet. He'd only been with the sleazy sweet butts who hung around the club. None of them had ever complained about his size. But none of them were as delicate as Janet. He didn't want to hurt her accidentally.

He closed his eyes, not wanting to think about that.

Not wanting to think about anything but the way she felt.

She was tight but her body was allowing him in a little deeper with every stroke. He was going slowly even though he wanted to unleash himself, to take her roughly until he poured himself into her.

Maybe later.

She was making tiny whimpering sounds beneath him, mewling like a little kitten. Unnff... God she felt good. Nothing in his worthless life had ever made him feel a tenth of this pleasure. Not even close.

She clenched down on him as he was pulling out and he lost control for a split second, driving in as deep as he could go.

"Yes, Jack! Yes!"

He stared down at her, unsure. But it was written all over her face. She wanted what he wanted. He moaned and started pumping his hips into her. His shaft was sliding in and out of her sweet hole with ease now. With every stroke her walls massaged and squeezed him.

It wouldn't be long now.

He increased his tempo as he felt her body start to convulse beneath him. Her cries grew louder, spurring him on. He worked his cock inside her like a machine, pistoning in and out, harder and faster by the second. Suddenly he stopped and pushed himself inside her as far as he could go.

His cock gave a mighty jump. He moaned as he felt his seed erupt from his head, filling her up. He thrust into her a few more times as her body pulled at him, sucking him deep again.

Then he collapsed.

Jesus.

If he'd known it could be like that, he would have taken her the first time he wanted to. That very first night at the club. He would have done anything to be insider her.

He hoped she would let him do it again.

He rolled off of her and pulled her into his arms, staring at the ceiling. She snuggled against his chest in a way that suggested there was no place else she'd rather be. He allowed himself the luxury of thinking- hoping- she might let him keep her.

She might stay.

A cool drop of water hit his chest. What the- He laid back again when he realized she was crying. She wasn't crying because of him was she? He never wanted to make her cry again.

"What am I going to do Jack? I can't go home."

He squeezed her. Not crying because of him then. Good.

"I know."

"They don't love me."

"They're idiots."

"How do you know?"

"I met them."

He raised an eyebrow at her and she nearly burst out laughing. He was almost offended by the look of shock her face at the discovery that he had a sense of humor after all. Instead he decided that it was time to make love to her again.

Before she changed her mind.

But slower this time.

Much slower.

****

"I want to see you dance."

Janet was cuddled up in his lap on one of the deck chairs, watching the sun go down. He lifted her up and set her on her feet, facing him. Then he sat back down again.

Her eyes widened as he stared at her expectantly.

"Really dance."

She inhaled and exhaled shakily.

"I haven't danced in so long, Jack."

"So?"

"There's no music."

He just waited. She felt so awkward in front of him suddenly. What if she wasn't any good at it anymore? What if he laughed at her. She peeked at him shyly. He lifted the corner of his mouth the teeniest bit. For Jack, that was a pretty big smile.

"Okay."

She took a deep breath and moved back on the deck. She'd perform the part of Giselle when she reappears as a spirit to save her lover. Of course, she couldn't do it full out without toe shoes, but she could mark it out. She'd have to be careful on the rough wood deck.

She tuned out everything around her and heard the music in her head. She rose gracefully as the spirt of Giselle into a full arabesque, one leg pointing high in the sky behind her. Then she fell into the dance, abbreviating the turns and leaps but doing most of the footwork. The dance was one of lost love and redemption. She felt all the emotions of the dance filling her up and spilling out as she spun in revoltade after revoltade, finally sinking to the ground as Giselle returned to her grave.

Janet lifted her head to see Jack watching her with tears in his eyes. He lifted his hands and clapped, slow and hard, until she ran into his arms. He pulled her into his lap and kissed her.

"You are so beautiful."

She snuggled deeper into his chest. She hadn't danced in so long. She'd been afraid to. But here and now, it had felt right somehow.

She felt wonderful. Everything in this moment was perfect. She'd never felt so safe and secure in her life. Until Jack's next words brought reality crashing back down on her.

"Let's go home."

She nodded sadly. If that's what he wanted, she would do it. She'd do anything for him at this point. The last thing she wanted was to leave this beautiful place... The place where she'd finally had Jack all to herself.

It wasn't just that she didn't want to go home.

She didn't have one.

10

Jack pulled up to Janet's parents house. Her bedroom window was boarded over. Good. He hoped everyone knew why. Then the neighbors would know what sick people were living there.

"I don't want to go in there."

He turned to look at Janet. She looked so small all the sudden. Like a lost little girl. He tried to smile reassuringly.

"So don't. I'm just going to get some clothes for you. Though you do look pretty cute in my shirts."

"Oh."

"Did you think I would take you back here? After what they did?"

"I- I don't know what to think. Or expect."

He leaned forward and pressed his lips to her forehead.

"You can stay with me for as long as you want."

When he pulled back she was staring up at him with an odd look. He never seen that look in anyone's eyes before. It told him that he was the most important person in the world to her. He inhaled sharply. Then she blinked and it was gone.

Jack got out of the car and walked up to the front door, pounding it with his fist. He didn't care what time in the morning it was. After a minute Janet's father opened the door. He was bleary eyed. Clearly he'd just been woken up.

Jack shouldered him out of the way and walked straight to Janet's bedroom. He found a duffle bag in the closet and started shoving clothes into it. He opened a drawer and grinned at all the frilly lady items inside. He emptied the entire drawer into the bag and then moved to the next drawer.

Then he looked at the hanging clothes. Janet sure had a lot of fancy stuff.

He was rummaging around for something else to put her clothes in when he saw her father standing hesitantly in the door.

"Is she alright?"

"I need another bag."

"I'll get one. Is she?"

He nodded brusquely and the man disappeared, coming back with a garment bag and another large suitcase. He helped Jack as he packed Janet's things.

In the end, Mr. Mahoney ended up carrying half of her stuff out to the car with Jack. He teared up when he saw Janet in the passenger seat.

"Thank God you are alright."

Janet didn't say anything as they loaded the car. She stared straight ahead until Jack was in the drivers seat. She glanced at him for reassurance. He nodded. Janet turned to her father.

"Goodbye dad."

That was it. She turned away from the open window and Jack pulled away from the curb.

****

Janet stared out the window of the SUV at the huge metal sign that read 'JH Bikes.' Jack owned his own custom bike shop. He'd said he was good at fixing things. How had she not known about that?

From the looks of it, business was booming.

"I live on the top floor. There's a couple of empty floors up there too. It's not much but-"

"Are you kidding? It's awesome."

He looked relieved. She was coming to realize that he did care what she thought. Very much so. She smiled and got out of the car.

"Jack!"

A couple of guys were in the shop working. They raised their hands in greeting, looking at Janet curiously. Jack scowled and grabbed a handful of her stuff. She looked at his hand gripping her luggage. He could carry a lot with those huge hands.

That wasn't the only huge thing he had... she blushed, remembering making love with him that third time on the deck in the open air. He'd laid a blanket down on the hard wood and then he'd taken her twice. Fast the first time and then slow the second. That was four times they'd done it in one night. She was a little bit sore to tell the truth. But she didn't care.

Not one bit.

She followed him through a large metal door to an industrial elevator. He pulled the gate down behind them and threw the lever, watching carefully as they rose three stories. There were a lot of empty floors.

"Who owns this place?"

He glanced over his shoulder at her. "I do."

She raised her eyebrows and looked around.

"This elevator has a lot of possibilities."

He turned sharply and threw the lever. His mouth opened as he gathered her meaning. He took a deep breath and shook his head to clear it.

Was he blushing?

He started the elevator again.

"I'm going to remember that you said that."

She felt a funny little dip in her stomach at his words. They sounded like a promise.

The elevator stopped at the third floor and he raised the gate. Janet looked around in wonder. It was an enormous loft. The kind you see in Magazines about New York Artists. It was clean and spartan, with very little furniture. There were a few things here and there, a table and chairs under a long bank of windows. Bookshelves. Jack read books?

And there against the back wall was an enormous bed. It looked like a California King. Of course it was. A big man like him needed a big bed. It rested on some sort of platform built out of wood.

"I can get more stuff."

She looked at him curiously. He'd set her bags down and was watching her carefully. She ran her fingers over the back of a heavy wooden chair.

"It's beautiful Jack. I love the furniture. Where did you get all of this?"

"I made it."

She stared at him, momentarily dumbstruck. Then she smiled at him. He looked so serious and she wanted to make him smile again. His smile made him light up.

"Is there anything you can't do?"

He smiled, an adorably lop sided grin. For a split second she saw the little boy toiling in the kitchen. Unloved and uncared for. Her heart broke a little bit.

"I can't dance."

She laughed. She couldn't help it. Then she saw the metal staircase leading upwards.

"What's that?"

He took her hand and led her towards it.

"Come on. I want to show you something."

****

Jack pushed open the door to the roof. He'd only just begun building the deck up here in his spare time. But it was going to be spectacular when he finished. He stole a look at Janet to see what she thought.

She was smiling and spinning in a circle.

"You can see the mountains from here!"

He walked over to a tarp and lifted it to reveal his tools.

"It's not done yet."

She was giving him an odd look suddenly. She looked... suspicious.

"How many girls have you brought up here, Jack?"

"None. Not ever."

She sighed and hugged her chest with her arms. He stared at her long, beautiful legs. She was still wearing his t-shirt. He hoped she'd make a habit of wearing his shirts around the house. He took a deep breath and exhaled.

Here goes nothing.

Here goes everything.

"I want you."

She tossed her head in that familiar proud way. He grinned.

"You've already had me, remember? Four times. I thought you didn't do repeat customers."

She arched her eyebrow at him, daring him to answer that.

"No Janet. I mean I want you. Permanently."

Her eyes opened wide.

"You do?"

He nodded and smiled at her uncertainly, just a little bit worried about what she might say. That was a lie. He was worried. A lot.

She was beside him in an instant, laughing as she planted tiny kisses all over his face. He leaned down and took her lips. Ten minutes later he had a thought.

They should finish unloading the car so he could take it back to Dev.

His body molded itself to hers instinctively as she pressed herself into his with equal force.

Dev was going to have to wait.

11

Devlin sat at the bar at the clubhouse, killing time before Kaylie got off of work. He waved as Jack walked into the room and crossed to the bar. He laid Dev's keys on the counter.

"Thanks."

"No problem man! I was psyched to try out your sick ride."

Donnie leaned on the bar and leered at them suggestively, handing Jack a ginger ale.

"Speaking of rides..."

He let the words hang suggestively, making Jack scowl furiously. Devlin couldn't help but laugh and slap Jack's back.

"How's Janet? Kaylie's been out of her mind with worry."

Dev and Donnie stared at Jack as a slow smile lit up his face. They'd never seen him smile that like before. Hell, they'd never seen him smile *period.*

He downed his ginger ale and nodded. Then he walked out of the clubhouse. An odd out of tune sound followed him as he left.

Dev glanced at Donnie who was staring at Jack with his mouth open.

"Dev, please tell me I've lost my mind...."

Devlin laughed at Donnie, who seemed to be at a loss for words for once in his life. He wished he had a camera to capture the awestruck look on Donahue's face.

"Is Jack humming?"

Safe In His Arms

By

Joanna Blake

Chapters

Donnie sat in one of the booths and stared out into space. Actually, that's not true. He blinked and realized he was doing it again.

He'd been watching her. Just like he did every time he came into the diner.

Sally.

She was the quiet, mousy waitress that worked with Kaylie most every shift. In fact, she seemed to practically live at the damn place. Almost every time he came into Mae's he found his eyes drawn to her irresistibly. He tried to look away but he always ended up with his eyes following her as she worked.

The damnedest part was, he couldn't figure out *why.*

It's not that Sally wasn't pretty. She was definitely a cutie, in an extremely wholesome way. But Donnie liked his women uber feminine and flouncy. This girl, with her blond hair constantly pulled back in a ponytail, long bangs concealing her eyes and no makeup, was practically fading into the background. Never mind the fact that he couldn't get a glimpse of her body. Lord knows, he had tried. But with her loose fitting uniform and fuzzy old cardigan, it was impossible to tell what sort of figure she had hidden under there. He frowned. She was always wearing that thing. Even in July. She kept her apron tied loosely as well. The woman could be a swimsuit model or a wraith for all he knew.

And yet he watched her.

Even stranger was how much he enjoyed it.

Maybe it had to do with how gracefully she moved around the diner. Or those big eyes of hers. A couple of times he'd caught her eye and felt a pure jolt of energy sizzling between them. But she always looks away too fast for him to be sure.

She glanced his way and blanched, growing even paler if that was possible. He shifted his eyes away momentarily and then watched as she scurried into the back. He stood and stretched.

"Gonna hit the head."

Dev just nodded, distracted by watching his old lady fill up the salt and pepper shakers. Donnie rolled his eyes. Man, Dev was whipped.

Devlin was the head of the club and was strong willed as hell. But when it came to his woman, he was putty. It was funny to watch, sure. But Donnie promised himself he would never let a woman make him feel that way.

Jack was just as bad. Ever since he'd known him Jack had been silent and grim. A couple of months ago that had all changed abruptly. Jack was frequently seen smiling. Donnie even heard him laugh once or twice.

Jack's transformation was even funnier than Dev's.

Women.

He shook his head and pushed open the swinging door to the back. They'd been teasing him that he was next. No way man. Donnie wasn't the settling down type.

He was walking down the hallway toward the bathroom when he heard it.

Singing.

Not just singing. *Beautiful* singing. It sounded like an angel. It was a sweet country song that he was sure he'd heard on the radio before but he couldn't quite place it. Something about Sundays and maydays.

He followed the sound to the stock room where Sally was standing on a step stool stacking boxes of napkins. He could hear her voice even better now. He was practically frozen in place by the shock of it. She should be singing professionally, not waiting tables in a tiny place like this.

Incredible.

He stood there listening to her sing, completely enraptured. She was an amazing singer but it was more than just that. There was a sweet sadness in her voice that pierced him to the core. He stood there mesmerized as she sung softly to herself and leaned forward to stack boxes of paper napkins on the shelf.

The other bonus was that he finally had a really good view of her legs.

They were good legs.

Really good.

He must have made a sound of appreciation because she turned suddenly and gasped. Shit, he hadn't meant to scare her. Her eyes widened as she tottered back and forth on the stool. Donnie realized she was about to fall a split second before she did.

He caught her against him and fell backwards against a stack of boxes, knocking them over. His arms were around her so she came with him, landing squarely on top of him.

Dear God.

Donnie was in shock as he stared into the biggest green gold eyes he'd ever seen. Hazel. They were hazel. How had he not noticed that?

And he finally had his answer about her body.

Phen-fucking-nominal.

He grinned at the girl lying sprawled on top of him. Her big, luscious breasts were crushed against his chest. Her waist was tiny under his hands and... he let them slide down a bit to feel her rounded hips and bottom. Accidentally of course.

Jesus, the woman was stacked.

"You alright sweetheart?"

She made a little sound of outrage and pushed against his chest.

"Let me up."

He grinned and squeezed her waist.

"What's your rush?"

She frowned at him and wiggled out of his grasp. Damn, he really hadn't wanted to let her go. She brushed herself off and stared down at him, looking annoyed.

"Can you help me up?"

He held up his hand and made his best puppy dog eyes at her. She looked at his hand distrustfully before grabbing it to hoist him up. Damn, she was a suspicious little thing!

He made sure to overshoot so he could get close to her again, landing on his feet up with his chest pressing against her body. He slid his arms around her waist to stabilize himself and smiled down at her. She gasped and jumped backwards. He raised his eyebrows at her with an unspoken invitation.

If it wasn't obvious enough the first time.

Usually that's all it took for Donnie to get a girl on her back. Of course the girls he messed around with were mostly hangers on who showed up at the club night after night, not shy little waitresses. He'd also never done it in a storage room. There was plenty of room though. Especially if he bent her over... He was already hard at the thought of it.

Or not.

Sally did not look like she was picking up what he was putting down come to think of it.

In fact, the girl looked even angrier. She was obviously not used to male attention. That's all it was. Once she got over the shock that Donnie wanted her, she'd come around.

God, he hoped so.

"You guys okay?"

Kaylie stood at the door to the storage room, surveying the mess. He glanced over at Sally. She looked ready to jump out of her skin.

"I fell and-"

"I caught her."

Sally yanked her apron off and crumpled it into a ball.

"I'll clean this up in the morning Kaylie. Do you mind closing up? I just- I have to go- sorry."

Donnie got goosebumps just listening to her talk. Her voice was beautiful, melodious, even just yammering about closing up. He grinned at her dopily. Then she shot him a furious glance and pushed out of the stockroom. They heard the little bell over the front door jingle.

"Jeez, what happened Donnie?"

He smiled at Kaylie.

"Nothing. She just slipped. Here, I'll fix this mess."

He didn't know why, but he didn't like the thought of Sally having to do this all by herself.

"Okay Donnie. That's nice of you to do."

She turned to go but he stopped her.

"Hey Kaylie, why don't you invite your friend to the barbecue on Saturday."

"Who, Sally?"

He smiled and nodded.

"Tell her to wear something cute."

"Are you sure Donnie? She seems kind of quiet for you."

"What, don't you like her?"

Kaylie gave him a look that would have cut glass.

"I like her a lot Donnie. I just don't want you messing with her head. She's not really your type anyway."

He just laughed.

"Maybe my type has changed."

****

Sally stared at herself in the mirror. She sighed, pulling her button down shirt forward to cover her breasts. Not that they were easy to hide. She'd blossomed at twelve and they had just kept coming. She tried yanking the top underneath up. If she left it open over her pretty pink camisole, you couldn't see how big they were from the sides. Or how tiny her waist was. She had the sort of figure that attracted attention a little too easily. Unfortunately she didn't have a potato sack laying around.

It would have to do.

When Kaylie had invited her to the barbecue, she'd specifically mentioned leaving her cardigan at home. She'd smiled to show she was joking but Sally knew it held a kernel of truth. She was unnaturally attached to her grandmother's old sweater. Maybe it was time to retire the ratty old thing. It made her feel safe though.

Hidden.

She stood up straight. No more. She'd been here for over a year now. It was plenty of time to learn how to protect herself. This town was her home now. It would be okay to go out and socialize a little bit.

It would.

Besides he would be there.

Donnie

She felt a tremor of butterflies go through her. Donnie was a frequent presence at Mae's. Whether he was outside, lounging on his bike while waiting for Dev and Kaylie, or inside, lounging in one of the booths and eating apple pie.

The guy loved to lounge.

She knew he was a biker and bad news. Those guys didn't treat women right. Kaylie's boyfriend Devlin seemed to be the exception. He was absolutely devoted to her. And Jack with his new girlfriend Janet. But they were smart girls. Brave and always standing up for themselves. For someone like her, it was better to stay away.

That didn't mean she couldn't look though, did it?

With his dark hair and piercing blue eyes, Donnie was gorgeous. He was almost too pretty to be a biker. She'd even heard some of the other guys give him shit about it. She'd nearly laughed out loud at the sour look on his handsome face.

Yeah, Donnie could have easily modeled with his looks. Never mind being tall and incredibly well built. The man was pure muscle. Not that he would ever notice someone like her.

The old her, yes. But the new, mousy, afraid little ghost? Doubtful.

She'd have to resign herself to her extremely active fantasy life and leave it at that. After the other night she had something new to add to the pot; the ways his arms had felt around her. And the way he smelled. And the moment when he looked at her the way a man looks at a woman he wants to kiss.

She'd seen that look before.

Of course, they always started out looking at her like that. Before the looks turned to disgust. Before they started using their fists.

She shook off the thought and reached for one of her old sparkly pink lip glosses without thinking. She immediately snatched her hand back as if the pink tube were a poisonous snake. No. She would wear her hair down and leave the cardigan at home but she would *not* wear makeup. She didn't want anyone to actually *look* at her. She reached for her good old cherry chapstick and slipped it into her jeans pocket. The designer jeans were from her old life. They were sexy and hugged her rear tightly but that couldn't be helped. She couldn't afford a whole new wardrobe on a waitresses salary.

At least these didn't have rhinestones on them like most of her other ones did.

****

"She said she was coming?"
Donnie knew he sounded like a chick but he couldn't help it. Kaylie was being nice enough not to mention it, though he had seen her hiding a smile

the fourth or fifth time he'd asked.

"Yes. Well, she said she'd probably stop by. I don't think she goes out much."

He frowned. Why was that? She certainly wouldn't have trouble finding a date. Even with her dowdy clothes and lack of makeup, she was a very, *very* pretty girl.

"What does she do when she's not working?"

Kaylie shrugged.

"I'm not sure really. She works a lot of shifts. I know she likes to reads a lot of books too."

"Books?"

"Yeah, they are these pieces of paper with words on them, all stuck together."

Jack and Janet laughed from their perch on the picnic bench nearby. Great, he was hoping no one had heard that. Those two always seemed to be in their own world these days.

"That's it?"

"Yeah. Sally doesn't really talk about herself too much. Oh I know! She said she wanted to get a dog."

Now Donnie rolled his eyes. She wasn't giving him much to go on. It didn't really matter anyway. He wanted her. In fact, he couldn't remember wanting a woman this badly ever before in his life.

So, it was more or less a foregone conclusion that little Miss Sally Adams was going to be in his bed. Soon. Not one woman on Gods green earth had ever been able to resist him yet. Usually, he didn't even have to do anything. Well, he did have this one move he used a lot. Not a move so much as a smile. He'd turn on the charm, flash the pearly whites and BAM, the panties came off.

He'd brushed his teeth twice this morning just to make sure they sparkled.

"She's here."

He straightened up and looked toward the clubhouse entrance. The entire parking lot had been turned into areas for cooking and eating. And of course, drinking. A lot of people were drunk already.

He felt like the air got sucked out of his lungs when he saw her. She looked... different out of her uniform. Beautiful really. And nervous. Very, very nervous. No wonder, with all the drunk people horsing around. He made a beeline right for her.

She was wearing an open button down shirt over a tank top and tight jeans. Her beautiful blond hair was down, tumbling like spun gold over her shoulders.

Spun gold? Who the hell was he?

Donnie told himself to get it together or he was going to make an ass of himself. No- even *more* of an ass of himself. He decided he'd be friendly but he wouldn't hang all over her. He'd let *her* come to *him.*

As he got closer he saw the lacy little camisole she was wearing. His mouth dried up as he stood over her and stared down her shirt. He didn't mean to, but he was tall and she was a tiny little thing. Well, not *all* of her was tiny.

Jesus, what a rack!

He couldn't look away for a minute. The tops of her luscious mounds were visible from up here in a way that made his body react instantaneously. A man could get lost in there. He had never seen anything so sensual in his life. Shy little Sally and her lacy underthings.

Damn.

She stared up at him, startled. He realized he was standing there like a dolt. So he smiled. She looked even *more* alarmed if that was possible.

"Hey."

"Hi."

"Come on, Kaylie's over here."

She smiled at him nervously so he took her arm and started shouldering people out of the way. He glared at anyone who even glanced at Sally. And then he glared more when he saw that Kaylie, Janet *and* Jack were all laughing at him.

He was used to being funny. He was *not* used to being amusing.

At least Devlin was out on an errand. He was picking up the fancy mustard Kaylie liked. Devlin wouldn't make fun of him for this ridiculous crush.

That's all it was. A crush. Right?

The girls greeted Sally warmly and pulled her up onto the picnic table between them. He felt ridiculous, standing there and watching her, not sure what to say.

He never had a problem knowing what to say.

"So, do you want a beer?"

She nodded shyly and he smiled, feeling much more at ease. A beer. He could get her a beer.

****

Sally sat on the wood picnic table sandwiched between Kaylie and her friend Janet. Donnie had been acting strange, overly solicitous. It was throwing her off guard.

He was acting like they were on a date.

"So did you figure out why we invited you yet?"

Kaylie was smiling at her as if she had a secret. Sally shook her head and tried not to stare as a biker threw a half naked woman over his shoulder and carried her into the clubhouse.

"Other than the pleasure of your company of course."

Janet winked at her. She felt her cheeks warming up suddenly. She knew what they were going to say. Of course. It all made sense now.

Donnie.

He was walking toward her with two beers and a determined look on his face. Her stomach seemed to drop out of her body and hit the ground. How could it be that her forbidden fantasy, the one thing she wanted but could never risk having, was now coming to life?

Damnit.

Why did it have to be him? Anyone else she could brush off. In fact, she did on a regular basis. Even without the makeup and fancy clothes she used to wear, she seemed to attract more than her fair share of male attention. She groaned inwardly. She should have gotten a fake wedding band when she first moved to town. Or made up a boyfriend. One that was big and mean and in the military.

"He likes you."

Kaylie leaned close and whispered the obvious. It sent a shiver of pure excitement down her spine. Immediately followed by dread.

Oh no. This was bad.

He handed her a beer and leaned against the edge of the picnic table, staring at her intently. He looked hungry.

And he was looking at her like she was something good to eat.

This was very, *very* bad.

She had to get out of here. Now.

"Thank you."

He grinned again. He looked like she'd just thanked him for saving a kitten from a tree. Way too proud of himself.

And way too sure he was going to get what he was after.

Her.

Sally felt a flush of arousal as his eyes slid down her body. She was under no illusions that he just wanted to get her into bed. She was sure he had women throwing themselves at him all the time. Looking around this place, there were tons of hot girls and more than a few were looking his way.

But Donnie was in for a surprise.

Sally was not going to lay down for him. No matter how much she might like to. If she was honest with herself, she wanted to a lot.

She sipped the beer, wondering how long it would take before she could leave without attracting more attention. She wracked her brain for an excuse- something that wouldn't offend her friend. She really did like Kaylie. If things were different, she would tell her everything. But as it was, she couldn't be too open, not even with the few girlfriends she'd made in this town.

Who was she kidding? She had one friend. Janet was nice but they'd only hung out a few times. Mae was her boss, even though Sally liked her a lot, it wasn't that kind of relationship. Kaylie was it. And now Sally was going to ruin it by running out of here.

She'd be all alone again.

She felt tears welling up in her eyes suddenly.

Coming here had been a mistake. She started to stand and make her excuses when there was a big commotion toward the gate.

Devlin was here. He was grinning as he jumped up on a table in the middle of the courtyard.

****

Kaylie was watching Devlin with a bemused look on her face. What was he up to now? He waited for everyone to quiet down before speaking. It was so quiet that he didn't even have to raise his voice.

"As all of you know, I met a very special lady about a year ago. She's been my old lady ever since but now it's time to make it official."

Her stomach did a funny little flip. What was he doing? Was he proposing to her?

He smiled at her and then opened his mouth and said something that made her doubt her sanity.

"We're getting married!"

A thunderous cheer went up from the crowd. Except from her. Kaylie noticed that Janet, Jack, Donnie and Sally all looked as shocked as she was. She felt sick, like the world was tilting on it's axis.

"Oh my god."

White hot anger filled her body, replacing the shock. Then she felt like bursting into tears. She had to get out here, go somewhere private where she could cry. She glanced around for an escape route but people were already starting to crowd the picnic table to offer congratulations.

"I need to get out of here."

"I'll go with you."

She nodded, grateful for Sally's support. Kaylie looked around wildly. They'd have to go in through the clubhouse and out the back. Then they could sneak around around to the other side. Otherwise they'd be swarmed by well wishers.

Or worse yet, Devlin himself.

"Come on, this way."

Sally set her beer down and followed Kaylie as she murmured 'sorry, bathroom' over and over again. They were inside the cool building and out the back in less than five minutes.

"What now?"

"If we go around the far side, where the dumpster is-"

"Kaylie?"

She turned to see Devlin standing behind her. He looked utterly baffled. And hurt.

Darn it.

"What's wrong sweetheart?"

She closed her eyes. There was no holding back now. No running away to lick her wounds and gather her thoughts. It was now or never.

"Weren't you even going to mention this to me before telling the rest of the world?!?"

"I thought you liked surprises."

"Devlin, listen to me. You've been making decisions for me since the day we met. But this is something I have to decide for myself. Besides, I am too young to get married!"

"I thought you wanted this. You said you wouldn't move in with me until we were married."

She just stared at him, mouth agape. How could he miss the point so completely?

"Don't you want to marry me sweetheart?"

He looked at her with those big green eyes of his and she almost melted. Almost.

"It's not that Devlin. It's just- I'm so young. And you didn't even ask me! A girl wants to be proposed to!"

"I'm asking you now."

She felt tears welling up in her eyes. How badly she wanted to say yes- to just forget the high handed way he'd asked her- no, *told* her.

"I'm sorry I just- I need some time to think."

His face was white as she backed away from him. She'd never seen him look like that. He looked lost.

She grabbed Sally's hand and ran.

****

Sally followed Kaylie around the side of the building and through the crowd around the front gate. Then suddenly they were out on the street. She breathed a sigh of relief as they hurried down the sidewalk. She didn't like crowds.

Not anymore.

"You okay?"

Kaylie was walking fast with tears rolling down her face. Sally put her hand on her younger friend's shoulder.

"Weren't expecting that, huh?"

"How could he? The day you get engaged is supposed to be one of the happiest days in your whole life!"

"I'm sorry Kaylie."

Sally felt awful for her friend. What a mess. But she was glad to get out of the clubhouse and away from Donnie. Not that she didn't like him. It was that she liked him *too* much.

That was dangerous for someone like her.

He was dangerous.

A tough guy like him was just the sort who would manhandle a woman. He was a criminal after all. Weren't all bikers? And she'd seen the way they treated the scantily clothed women at the barbecue. They'd been pure cavemen, taking their pick of the girls without asking. That's what Devlin had done to Kaylie, even if he'd been sweet about it.

That's what Donnie wanted to do to her.

She shivered suddenly, the image of Donnie throwing her over his shoulder and taking her somewhere private to have his way with her. Her body was hot suddenly. She wouldn't mind that so much. What she minded was what happened *after*.

First he'd get used to her, start taking her for granted. Then he'd start barking little commands at her. Telling her what to eat, where she could go, what she could wear. Then came the insults... and finally the fists.

She'd rather be alone than go through that again.

Maybe she was fooling herself, thinking she'd be safe here.

Maybe it was time to find a new town.

"Sorry about all of this Sally. I think I need to go home. My mom will be home from work soon."

"Don't apologize to me. I was ready to leave anyway. I have a class this afternoon."

"Oh okay. I'm glad you came, anyway. I'll see you at the diner later this week?"

"Yes. Have a good night Kaylie. Call me if you want to talk."

"I will. And thanks."

Sally watched Kaylie turn down the street that she lived on. Sally's house was just a couple of blocks further. She looked behind her suddenly, feeling like someone was watching her. She shivered suddenly as her arms broke out in goosebumps.

But there was no one there.

2

Donnie and Jack sat in silence in the slowly emptying parking lot. Janet had left shortly after Kaylie and Sally to go see if her friend was okay. Meanwhile Dev was in the clubhouse bar, slowly drinking himself into oblivion.

"What a disaster."

Jack just nodded. No one had expected Kaylie to run off like that. Dev must be destroyed right now.

Donnie knew it was selfish of him but he was more upset that Kaylie had taken Sally with her. He'd barely had a chance to talk to her at all.

He considered going in to keep his friend and leader company. But the thought of drinking heavily was unappealing to him. He wanted to be sitting with a certain pretty lady, eating chicken wings. Or not. He'd really rather be tasting her right now... those sweet lips... her earlobes... then lower...

He should go see if she was okay. Offer to take her out another time. He had a vague idea of where she lived, just from seeing her walking around town. It wasn't in the best part of town, that much was certain. It was odd, all the little things he'd noticed about her in the past year. All without realizing he was doing it.

Kind of like a stalker actually.

He stood up abruptly.

"I gotta go."

"Okay. I'll keep an eye of Dev."

"Thanks man. I'll check in later."

He was out the gate and on his bike in less than a minute. He pulled his helmet on and smiled. He never had chicks on the back of his bike but he kept a spare helmet back there just in case. He kind of hoped he would need it.

****

Sally pulled the hoodie down over her face and walked faster. If she could get there in 5 minutes, she could make the 4 o'clock class at the dojo. You weren't allowed in if you were late. Jerry Davis, who owned the place, was very strict.

Then again, he always made exceptions for Sally.

She did her best to ignore the fact that Jerry pretty openly had a crush on her. After almost a year though, it was hard not to notice the discounts, special attention and lingering looks. It's too bad he wasn't her type. He was blond and reasonably good-looking. A total jock. A nice guy with his own business. Exactly the kind of guy she should be going for. But he just didn't do it for her. He was too... boring. She hoped he never actually asked her out because she would hate to hurt his feelings.

After all, this place had changed her life.

Before taking classes she'd been weak, at the mercy of anyone stronger. Now she could at least stand up for herself, if not win, a fight with someone twice her size. Plus she had the element of surprise on her side.

No one expected a pretty little blond like her to whoop their butts.

She almost hoped she'd get a chance to use her new skills.

Almost.

She hustled and slid into class just before Jerry shut the doors. Good. She needed this today. She needed to feel empowered.

Jerry's eyes flicked over the seven students lined up. Oh no. An odd number. Sally knew what that meant.

"Sally, you'll spar with me."

She nodded and joined Jerry at the front of the classroom. She bowed and they began. Jerry was laser focused, challenging her at ever turn. That's until she took her work out jacket off.

Oops.

She regretted taking it off immediately.

She almost rolled her eyes at the way he was so distracted by her body. Her tight tank top and jogging pants, with the tiny glimpse of a hot pink jog bra was not standard gear for the dojo.

But Jerry did not seem to mind. In fact, he was barely paying attention to anything other than her torso. Or her butt. Or her legs. It was almost insulting how blatantly he was ogling her.

Then again, he was distracted so...

She got a direct hit to his chest, sending him stumbling. He landed against the wall and was on his feet in an instant, glaring at her.

Uh oh.

Jerry wasn't distracted anymore.

They sparred for the rest of the hour and a half class until she was exhausted and soaked in sweat. He challenged her at every turn, keeping her on her toes, really honing her instincts and technique. She was wiped out by the end, with jello for muscles.

It was tough as hell.

It felt awesome.

She was patting herself down with the towels Jerry kept at the front desk when she looked outside and saw him.

Donnie.

He was outside, lounging on his motorcycle with his long legs stretched out in front of him. He really did look like a model pretending to be a biker. But what was he doing out there in the dojo parking lot?

Oh god. He was...

Waiting for her.

"Friend of yours?"

She nearly jumped out of her skin from the voice behind her. Jerry was practically whispering in her ear. He was that close.

Too close.

She could feel his breath on the back of her neck. She stepped sideways toward the exit. Now she was getting annoyed. Couldn't the guy take a hint?

"Yes. He is."

"Be careful Sally. The Spawns aren't good guys you know. They don't treat women well."

Oh, and you would?

She gritted her teeth and forced herself to sound calm and most importantly- cool.

"I can take care of myself, Jerry."

She pushed the glass door and stepped out, almost missing the odd look Jerry was giving her. He didn't look like a nice guy in that moment. Not at all.

Donnie smiled and stood up as soon as he saw her. She squared her shoulders and walked over to him. She reminded herself that she had nothing to be afraid of. He was just a guy. A really, really hot guy, but a guy all the same.

Relax.

He was holding a helmet in his hands. She stared at them for a minute. His hands were huge compared to hers. He could do a lot of things to her with those hands... good and bad.

"Hi Sally."

"Hi Donnie. What are you doing here?"

"You disappeared so fast that I didn't get to talk to you."

"Sorry. Kaylie was pretty upset."

"Yeah, I gathered."

She just stared at him. He looked big and tough in all his leather but the look on his face was similar to what a puppy looked like when it wanted a bowl of kibble.

An enormous, muscle bound puppy with gorgeous blue eyes.

He looked utterly harmless.

She was afraid of him anyway.

He held out the helmet. There was another one on the seat behind him. Oh dear.

"Come on, let me give you a ride. It'll be fun."

"But I'm all sweaty."

He grinned at her in a way that made her heart start beating double time.

"It's hot out. So am I."

She did not want to get on that bike. She did not want to wrap her arms around him. She did not want to feel his body against her chest. She did not want to rub their sweaty bodies together.

She was such a liar.

"Okay."

He grinned and helped her put her helmet on. He was standing so close to her that they could have been kissing. She stared at his chest, ignoring the insistent tug she was feeling. The urge to look up at him and... just be.

She was just going for a ride, that was all.

Baby steps.

3

Donnie could not stop smiling. At first anyway. Sally was on his bike, letting him drive her around town. Her arms were clasped around his waist, which felt great, but he wanted more.

He picked up speed and her arms tightened, pulling her tight against his back. Jesus. He wished he had left his jacket at home. Then he could feel her body even better. As it was, he could barely think at all with her incredible breasts touching his back.

Maybe he should go a little faster...

He revved the motor and she was forced to hold him tighter, her body smushed against his, her legs spread wide behind him.

Oh God.

Donnie wasn't smiling all the sudden. No, he was fighting off the most intense arousal he'd felt in his entire life. He would lay money on the fact that his boner was hard enough to cut glass. Like a dick made out of diamonds. Thankfully, Sally couldn't see the huge bulge growing in his pants.

He headed out into the farmland that started just outside of town. The sun was just beginning to set and the country roads looked spectacular. Might as well give her a tour while he waited for his body to calm down. He had a feeling it might take a while.

After about twenty minutes they came to a hill that overlooked the setting sun. He pulled over so they could watch the sunset. He climbed off the bike and reached for her helmet.

She moved her head back subtly so he decided to leave it. He threw her a charming smile and pulled his helmet off. Then he offered her his hand. She stared at it for a minute before accepting his help off the bike.

He walked toward the lone tree on the hill before he realized she wasn't following him. So he went back. Sally was staring at him with her arms wrapped around her body.

"Are you cold?"

He pulled off his jacket and tucked it over her shoulders. She looked good in it, sweaty or not.

"What are we doing all the way out here?"

He shrugged.

"It's pretty. I thought you would like it."

"I thought you were just going to drive me home."

"What's the fun in that?"

It took a moment before he caught the look in her eyes.

Sally looked terrified. She looked away quickly but he had definitely seen it.

Fuck.

The girl was practically hyperventilating. Her eyes were full of tears. How had he missed that? He'd been too busy thinking with his dick.

"Was I going too fast?"

She didn't say anything. Just shook her head. Not the speed then. What the hell was wrong with her? Was she actually afraid of *him?*

"We can go home. I didn't mean to scare you."

"I'm not scared."

He frowned. She was lying. So much for his charm. And he really thought she was starting to warm up to him.

"Well, put the jacket on at least. It will keep you warm on the ride back."

She did as he asked and climbed stiffly back on the bike. He slid on in front of her. Way to go Donahue. Really winning over the ladies with your smooth moves. He rode slower on the way back, but he could still feel her against him. Her breasts brushed against his back with every turn. He groaned inwardly.

Talk about rubbing salt on the wound.

What the fuck was he supposed to do now?

****

Sally's breathing had slowed a little bit by the time he pulled up in front of her house. She yanked her hands back as soon as the bike stopped. She felt lightheaded, whether from the speed, his closeness, or the fear that had over taken her in the field, she wasn't sure. She was a bit wobbly as she climbed off the bike.

Donnie hastened to get off in front of her and give her his arm but she just shook her head, handing him his jacket and hurrying into the house. She fumbled with her keys until she had the door open and then collapsed against it. Hot tears spilled out over her face.

Safe. She was safe.

The confused look on Donnie's face was burned into her brain. Oh god, he must think she was insane!

Why did she have to ruin everything?

Her hands were shaking as she turned and slowly chained the door and threw the locks. She realized that for the first time in the past year, the first time since she had gone out on her own, the first time since she'd *escaped*, she hadn't locked the door behind her. Her guard must be down. Normally she did it the second she was inside the door. But she hadn't this time because she knew in her gut Donnie wasn't going to hurt her.

She knew it.

He hadn't taken her out into the country side to have his way with her and leave her bloody and bruised by the side of the road. He didn't want to beat her up, or insult her, or control her. He just seemed to like her for some obscure reason she couldn't figure out.

Damnit. She was a fool. Maybe they both were.

Oh well. Now she'd never know if her instincts were right about him. She felt pretty sure he'd be great in bed. And more importantly, he'd be good to her out of it. It was too late now that she'd acted like a lunatic.

One thing was for sure. If he hadn't scared her off, she had definitely scared him away. She felt a sense of loss at the thought that Donnie wouldn't be batting his ridiculously long eyelashes at her anymore.

She'd done it again. She'd insured that she was going to be all alone. Safe. But lonely.

She was definitely getting a dog.

****

Donnie slid behind the bar at the clubhouse. Dev was in his usual spot at the corner of the bar, with Jack sipping ginger ale beside him. They weren't talking.

Jack looked calm as usual. Dev... did not.

He was nursing what looked to be the most recent in a long line of beers. Empty shot glasses littered the bar around him.

A lot of shot glasses.

Donnie picked two of them up.

"Leave them!"

"I'm just getting us a refill Dev."

Dev grunted and watched bleary eyed as Donnie poured two shots of tequila and pushed one toward Dev. They did the shots and Donnie poured another round immediately.

"Shit man, you too?"

Donnie nodded grimly. Jack cracked a smile.

"Donnie striking out? That's a first."

"This is different."

"How so?"

"I like her."

Devlin rolled his eyes and Jack's smile got a little wider. Jack had been smiling a lot the last few months, since he and Janet got together. Lucky bastard. Donnie downed another shot.

"Like? Those are strong words for you, man."

"I take her for a ride and what does she do? She asks me to take her home. The bloody woman was scared of me for Christ's sake!"

"Scared of *you?* Now, that *is* funny."

Jack finished his soda and stood up.

"Well, I better get home to my woman."

Jack smiled and slapped Dev on the back. Hard. They stared at him as he walked out of the clubhouse. Donnie poured another two shots.

"Smug bastard."

"I hope his nuts fall off."

4

It was another busy night shift at Mae's. Sally was working alone, with Mae as backup. It used to be a shift she shared with Kaylie, but she was in school full time now. Sally didn't mind the extra work though. It was good to be busy. It gave her less time for worries. And regrets. God knows she had enough of those. She regretting meeting Carl, dating him, almost marrying him. She regretted letting him use her as a punching bag.

But most of all, she regretted pushing Donnie away.

Sally was on her hands and knees wiping up a spill when she saw them.

Big black motorcycle boots.

She looked up slowly, her eyes following those familiar long legs up to his belt buckle, over his tight t shirt that hugged all those bulging muscles, to that way too handsome face.

Donnie was at Mae's.

And he was smiling at her.

Her heart did a crazy little flip flop.

So she hadn't scared him off after all... Her first emotion was relief, followed by a nervous energy that set her blood zinging. She gave him a tentative smile and went back to picking up the broken pieces of porcelain. She hurried behind the counter and washed her hands, trying to buy time to think, to calm down, to erase the bright pink that was suddenly tinting her cheeks.

He was sitting at the counter pretending to look at a menu when she turned around. He was definitely not looking at the menu though. He was looking at her. He gave her a lopsided grin when she caught him staring.

"Hi Sally."

Her mouth was dry as she walked over to him.

"Hi Donnie. So, um, what can I get you?"

Oh god, she sounded like a stupid teenager! What was happening to her?

It's like her brain shut off when he was around. Or at least, her IQ dropped a few points.

More than a few.

He was smiling at her like she was a genius though. Huh.

"What's good? Other than you, I mean."

She opened her mouth to speak but no words came out. Was he flirting with her? He was. He definitely was. Duh. The trouble was, she'd forgotten how to flirt back.

"The special is a reuben sandwich."

He made a face.

"Too messy. Besides, I don't want bad breath. Do you have any soup?"

She nodded slowly. He didn't want bad breath. That meant he wanted to kiss her, right?

"Chicken noodle or lentil."

He smiled as if he were genuinely excited.

"I love chicken noodle!"

She almost rolled her eyes at how ridiculous he was being. She ladled out some soup and busied herself with the other customers while he ate it. She snuck a few glances at him. Donnie was eating his soup verrrry slowly.

She almost laughed. He was about as subtle as a mack truck. The diner was starting to empty out when he was finally done. She came over to take his bowl.

"Can I get you anything else Donnie?"

He pulled out the menu again and started looking at it with exaggerated interest. This time she did laugh. He frowned at her, pretending to be annoyed.

"Yes. I will have..."

He slammed the menu shut.

"More soup."

She shook her head and took his bowl away, replacing it with a fresh bowl of soup. This time she gave him extra crackers. His eyes twinkled as he accepted them from her.

The man was ridiculous!

He was *adorable.*

She started cleaning up the diner since there were only a few customers left by now. Mae had left after the dinner crowd thinned out, as usual. She liked to be there to tuck her grandkids in whenever possible. There was only a half hour left until closing. Sally checked the salt and pepper and sugar shakers, and pulled any ketchup bottles that were running low. Normally she set up at a booth and refilled everything but this time she brought them to the counter.

It felt like a bold move considering how jumpy he was making her.

But this time it was jumpy in a good way.

Every time she glanced up from restocking the table condiments he was eating his soup. No, he was savoring it. But each time she bent her head again, she felt his eyes on her. In fact, she could actually feel heat where his gaze touched her skin. Her neck... her ear...

her cheek...

Her heart was going fast by the time she finished and started carrying things back to the tables.

Donnie leapt up to help her.

"I can do that."

"Does that mean you are actually finished with your soup?"

"Well, there are at least three or four bites left..."

She was giggling as they carried the bottles and shakers to the tables together. She was nearly ready to close up. There was just one thing. His bowl.

She walked over to the front and flipped the 'open' sign to 'closed.' Charlie poked his head out of the back and hollered.

"You about ready to go girl?"

She took a deep breath. She could ask Charlie to wait until Donnie left. But she didn't want to. She knew she was safe with him. It would be okay. She repeated it to herself a few times.

Everything was okay.

"No that's okay Charlie, you go home."

The door jingled as Charlie let himself out. She sighed and reached for the broom. She swept up quickly and then came back to the register to close it out. Donnie was staring at her with a serious expression on his face, his spoon still in his hand. He set it down and pushed the bowl away.

"I didn't mean to keep you late."

"It's okay. I'm almost done."

She reached for his bowl and he grabbed her hand.

"Sally-"

She froze, staring at his hand where it clasped hers. His hand was so big. He could kill her with that hand. He could do it without even trying. She raised her eyes to his, half expecting to see anger, or lust. But his clear blue eyes were earnest and kind.

She blinked. No one had looked at her that way in a long time. But that was how they got you, she reminded herself.

Carl had started out sweet too. So full of compliments and flattery. Always opening doors. Always helping her with her coat and guitar.

She looked away and the spell was broken. She pulled her hand loose and he let her go. Poor Donnie probably thought she was a freak. She took his bowl and spoon and disappeared into the kitchen. She stayed there for a few minutes, until the tears that were hovering behind her eyes finally retreated.

When she came outside he was gone, and a twenty dollar bill sat on the counter. That was quite a tip for two bowls of soup. He was being a gentleman she knew. He wasn't full of empty flattery. Maybe he really was different. Pretty soon he'd give up and go away. That was better for everyone right?

"Stupid. Why am I so stupid?"

****

Donnie was leaning on his bike,
hoping she wouldn't freak out when she
saw him waiting in the parking lot. He
was finally figuring out that Sally wasn't
afraid of him. She was afraid of
something else. He didn't care though.
He was going to figure out what it was
that was making her so jumpy.

And then he'd kill it.

He straightened up and smiled
reassuringly when she came out of the
diner. She locked up and turned, freezing
when she saw him. Then she smiled.

Thank God.

"I thought I'd give you a ride."

Sally chewed on her lip for a
minute, driving him absolutely insane.

"Not tonight okay Donnie? I just
want to walk, I could really use the air."

He shrugged.

"I'll walk you home then."

"You don't have to do that."

She walked out of the parking lot and onto the sidewalk. He jogged a bit to catch up, flashing her a megawatt smile. She gave him an exasperated look. She was so cute it he could barely stand it. He was glad she'd left that ratty old sweater at home.

"Are you following me Donnie?"

"Escorting you darlin'. Big difference."

She rolled her eyes and turned her head away, but not before he caught her smile. He had a big shit eating grin on his face as he followed her home like a puppy dog. He knew he was being ridiculous. But for some reason he just didn't care.

"Aren't you afraid to leave your bike?"

"Nobody would mess with a Spawn's ride in this town."

She didn't say anything for the next block or two. He didn't mind. He just liked looking at her. Finally they walked up to her tiny house. It was old and decrepit, but she'd planted some pretty roses in front. He followed her to the front stoop.

"This is me."

"I know. I drove you home remember?"

"Oh. Right, of course."

He leaned on the side of the house and smiled at her. He was going to get a kiss no matter how hard she made it for him. He had to know if she would feel as good as he thought she would.

Her eyes grew wide as he pulled her toward him. He lifted her chin and stared into those huge hazel eyes. Then she sighed and her eyes fluttered shut. That was the sign! The green light!

He couldn't wait. He kissed her like his life depended on it. Hell, maybe it did.

Her lips were so damn soft! He moaned as he angled his lips over hers. He nudged her lips apart and magically, she opened them for him. She felt so damn good in his arms as he used his tongue to tangle with hers.

Kapow! Jesus, the girl could kiss. It started slow but then they were kissing each other madly, his hands roaming down her back, her hands sliding down under his shoulders and gripping his waist.

Oh god.

Twenty minutes must have passed by the time he was stroking her sides, sneaking his hands forward to caress her breasts. She made a little mewling squeal of protest.

Damn it. What was the problem?

Oh crap. They were still outside.

With an effort he tore his mouth from hers and stared in shock into her eyes. She looked as surprised as he did by the passion of their kiss. He'd never kissed anyone like that in his life. Not even close. She wasn't looking at him though, she was checking the street. For what?

Was she afraid of the neighbors seeing them? Inviting him in would take care of that pretty easily. He had never wanted anything so badly as to be invited inside. Even if he was able to restrain the urge to take all her clothes off and bury himself in her. He just wanted to keep kissing her dammit!

But she was about to bolt again. He could see it a split second before she pulled away.

"Sally-"

She had her keys out and was unlocking a series of what looked like four or five deadbolts. That was weird. She glanced over her shoulder at him, barely making eye contact.

"I have to go- I... Good night Donnie."

Then she was inside. Gone, just like that. He stood aside her house, breathing heavily. The lights came on inside and he snapped out of it, pushing away and walking away from her house. Then he was trotting, then running.

He needed to get his bike and ride home.

He needed a God Damn cold shower.

****

Sally leaned against the door and put her hand over her mouth. She could still feel him there. Oh god- she could still feel him *everywhere.* She was hot and cold all over. She moaned, realizing how close she'd come to letting him into her bed.

No, not letting. She'd been on the verge of *dragging* him into her bed and making him stay there. What the hell was wrong with her? She felt like a teenager. Not that she'd ever experienced lust like this before.

That's all it was. Lust.

She turned and slowly started throwing the locks. Her baseball bat was leaning in it's regular spot by the front door. The mace was hidden under her couch cushion. There were brass knuckles in the kitchen drawer. Basically, she had weapons stashed all over the damn house. She shook her head. She didn't need them anymore.

Carl wasn't going to find her. It had been a year. The trail must be cold by now. Maybe he'd given up. Maybe it would be safe to let Donnie come inside next time.

She sank onto the couch and stared into space, the image of Donnie's face coming towards hers stuck in her mind's eye. He'd looked so sensual, so intent. She lay down on the couch and hugged one of the ratty old pillows to her chest.

Damn but that boy could kiss.

5

Sally was curled into a ball, trying to protect her face. Huge fists were flying toward her, beating her, hurting her. She was so scared. But she was also mad.

Leave me alone!

As soon as that thought came into her head, he seemed to sense it and redouble his efforts.

She took a hit to the side of her head, up against her ear. A ringing sound filled her head. Not her ears! She needed her ears! She felt herself sliding into unconsciousness but the hits kept coming. Her arms slid away from her face and she felt a hit land on her cheekbone.

Then darkness.

Sally woke up with a scream on her lips. She looked around her tiny house stupidly. She'd fallen asleep on the couch.

She got up slowly and did what she always did when she had the dream. She took the crowbar by her bed and walked through the house, checking every door and window. She looked under the bed, in the closets and into the basement.

And then she sat down with her guitar at the kitchen table and wrote a song. It was a pretty tune, full of heartbreak and hope. But it wasn't ever going to be a number one hit. She couldn't risk ever having anyone hear it at all. If she did that he would find her for sure. But it still soothed her to put her feelings into words and melody.

She was up the rest of the night, as usual. She cleaned the house and played her guitar a few more times. She even did her martial arts drills. Finally she gave in and made a pot of coffee in the old drip pot the landlord had left behind.

She could never sleep after one of those nightmares. No matter how many times she told herself it was a dream.

Just a dream.

But it wasn't really.

It was a memory.

****

Donnie knew he looked ridiculous. A big guy on a bike with a huge bouquet of flowers tucked into the front of his jacket. He wiggled his nose as one of the flowers brushed his face.

God, he hoped nobody saw him.

Then again, he didn't really care. As long as he could get into Sally's house. Dear God, he wanted her to let him in. On more than one level. He wanted to get her into bed obviously. Desperately. The woman had some sort of magic spell on him so that all he could think about was touching her, kissing her, holding her... and more.

But he also wanted to get to know her better. And even more than anything, he wanted to know what was making her so fearful. He had an overwhelming desire to protect her. To tell her everything was going to be okay. That he'd protect her, if she'd let him.

He was good at that. Protecting women. He'd learned early, helping his mom look after his little sister, Marie. He'd had to protect them both. He hadn't always succeeded, but as he got older, it got easier.

The old man hadn't stood a chance against an angry fifteen year old Donnie.

Mean old bastard.

Donnie pushed the thought of his father aside and readjusted the flowers. He hoped she wouldn't mind him just showing up like this but it couldn't be helped. He didn't have her damn phone number!

But he'd get it today. Damn straight he would.

He pulled up in front of her house. He felt a bit nervous as he walked up to her front stoop and knocked. He heard pattering little footsteps and smiled. Then he heard a chain being unhooked.

And another chain. And a couple of locks.

Damn, the place was like Fort Knox!

She peeked out from a sliver of the door. There was still some sort of chain on it. He smiled, even though the number of locks was throwing him. How had he not noticed that before?

"Hi Sally."

He grinned and held up the flowers.

"These are for you."

She just blinked at him like a tiny little owl. Probably figuring out that she had to open the door to accept the flowers. He felt a bit like a heel, knowing he was being pushy. But she was so damn elusive that he didn't really have a choice. If he wanted her, he was going to have to use every trick in the book.

And God Damn did he want her.

"Oh. Thank you."

She closed the door to unhook the chain and opened it up again, wider this time. He almost swallowed his tongue when he saw her. She was wearing a pink tank top and a pair of tight jeans.

Her feet were bare and her cute little toes were painted a sparkly purple color.

Jesus, the woman was trying to kill him.

He handed her the flowers while trying to send her a message telepathically.

Let me in let me in let me in let me in...

"Would you like to come in?"

He grinned so wide he felt like his face would split in two. Every inch he got closer to her felt like a triumph. He stepped inside and watched as she locked the door again. He was staring at her door as her busy little hands clicked each lock into place.

She had eight locks.

He felt a cold weight settling in the pit of his stomach.

"I'll just put these in water.... is something wrong Donnie?"   He tried to keep his face devoid of emotion. He was shocked at how angry he was at the thought of someone threatening a sweet little thing like Sally. *His* sweet little thing.

"Has someone been bothering you Sally?"

She blanched and took in a sharp little breath but didn't say anything. He was practically vibrating with the need to punch somebody's face in. Whoever it was that made her this afraid.

"Tell me and I'll take care of it."

"No- there's just been- a lot of break ins around here. I'm alone here so..."

She licked her lips nervously. She was lying. He knew it.

"I'll get a vase."

He followed her into the kitchen. It was faded yellow and white, run down but spotlessly clean. He saw a guitar leaning under the window by the table. The window had bars on it.

He looked back the way they had come. Bars on those windows too.

A can of mace on the counter top. *Fuck.*

"Would you like a cup of coffee?"

He nodded and she gestured to the kitchen table. He sat down. Five minutes ago he would have been negotiating to sit on the couch in the living room. Much easier to get horizontal on a couch.

But now... now he knew that something was very wrong here. Now he had other things on his mind.

"You play?"

She jerked her head around, staring at the guitar as if it was a ghost.

"Oh. Not really. I'm not very good."

He narrowed his eyes at her back. Now she was really lying to him.

"As good as you sing?"

She shrugged and went back to making the coffee. She turned around and smiled at him while it percolated.

"I've had five cups already. I should be bouncing off the walls."

"Late night?"

She shrugged again.

"I couldn't sleep."

He nodded. He hadn't slept much either. She looked pretty as a picture though.

A picture that was lying through her teeth.

He stood up and crossed the kitchen.

"Sally."

She looked alarmed as he took his jacket off and pulled his t shirt over his head.

"What are you doing Donnie?"

"Relax darlin' I just want to show you something."

She looked ready to run as he turned side ways and showed her the tattoo on his shoulder. He could tell the moment she saw it. It was the face of a pretty young girl. Underneath it said 'Marie.'

"She's beautiful."

He nodded gruffly, turning the other way.

"That's my sister. And this-"

He showed her his other tattoo. This was another woman, older but still lovely. Underneath it said 'Mom.'

"Is my mother."

"They'r beautiful Donnie. But I don't understand why-"

"Because."

He leaned toward her and put his arms on the counter, boxing her in.

"They are the reason my arms exist. To protect them. I couldn't do it at first. He was too big. But by the time I was fifteen I started fighting back. He never laid a hand on either of them again."

Her mouth opened. He could see tears forming in her eyes.

"I won't let anyone hurt you again Sally."

"How did you know?"

He leaned forward and kissed her forehead, then pushed off and went back to the table.

"Let's just say you remind me of her. My sister. She was always jumping at shadows."

"Oh. What happened?"

"To my dad? I finally beat him so bad that he took off, never to be seen from again. Marie though, she was too little. She took too many knocks in the head. Now she's... not the same."

He glanced up at her.

"Tell me who did this to you. Who hurt you bad enough to make you hide yourself away like this?"

She took a shuddering breath and turned away to pour their coffee. For a minute he thought she wasn't going to answer. When she did, the words came out broken, like they hurt coming out.

"My road manager. Carl. He ran my crew at first and then he was my fiancé."

"He hit you?"

She nodded, not looking at him.

"He did lots of things. Hitting was one of them."

Donnie saw black. Then red. Then black again. He forced himself to stay calm. He didn't want to scare her.

"Where is this joker?"

"I don't know. Back in Nashville probably. He said he'd come after me, but maybe he didn't mean it. I don't know. I keep meaning to get a dog. A big one."

"I don't want you to worry anymore. You have a big dog. Right here."

He made a fist and thumped it against his bare chest.

"No Donnie. If he does find me, he'll kill you. He said he was going to kill me too, if I ever ran off or if I ever..."

"If you ever found yourself a man?"

She nodded. Well no fucking wonder she was so skittish. He felt like a giant ass for kissing her outside the other night. She'd been looking for this Carl bastard. He almost hoped he did come looking for her. He'd be in for a big fucking surprise.

"Do you want sugar?"

He was on his feet again before he knew what he was doing, his hands reaching for her, spinning her to face him and taking her mouth in a kiss that scalded both of them. He could not stop kissing her, could not stop his hands from molding the curves of her body to his, could not stop wanting more.

He wondered if he took her to bed a couple of times if this unquenchable thirst for her would be satisfied. He doubted it. It would take a thousand times and he'd still want her. But maybe he'd be able to think about something else for five minutes.

Donnie knew he was in danger of falling for this girl. Hard. But he didn't care anymore.

He had her leg around his waist with his huge palms cupping her round little cheeks when he finally came up for air. They were both breathing heavily. One of her tank top straps had slipped off, revealing a smooth golden shoulder. He kissed her there, lightly. Then moved up her neck with small deliberate kisses until he reached her ear.

"I want you Sally."

She moaned a little bit as he pressed his erection forward, nudging her sex. She lifted her hands up and placed them on his chest.

And gently pushed him away.

"I can't Donnie. I'm sorry."

He stepped backwards, breathing heavily. He squeezed his hands into fists to keep himself from reaching for her.

"Don't you like me Sally?"

She crossed her arms over her chest and looked away.

"I just- I just want to be left alone. It's easier that way."

He stared at her for a minute, hoping she would relent. But she wasn't even looking at him. She looked small, like she was trying to shrink into herself and become invisible.

"Please Donnie."

He cursed under his breath and grabbed his shirt and jacket. He didn't wait for her to come and unlock the door. He clicked open lock after lock until the door opened. It was beautiful out- a

perfect balmy afternoon in late spring.
But he didn't care.

He didn't care about anything.

6

Sally had finally cried herself to sleep a couple of hours before she had to be at the diner for the morning shift. She was working a double for the third time that week. If she was at the diner, she didn't have to think about Donnie.

Or Carl.

She had hated him before, feared and despised him. But now she was even angrier than she'd been when he hurt her, when he stripped away her self esteem and stole her country music career out from under her boot heels.

Now he'd robbed her of Donnie.

No, Donnie was just a nickname. His name was Donahue. She didn't even know his real first name. And she was unlikely to ever get a chance to. She's sent him away time and again. There was no way he would want her now.

At the diner she was like a shark; in constant motion. If a shark stopped moving it would die. Sally felt the same way. If she stopped moving she'd have to face the mess she'd made of things. She'd have to face the prospect of being alone.

Forever.

She looked around Mae's after putting the mop away. The place was clean when she'd come in earlier that morning, but now it was cleaner. Spotless even. She sighed. It might be just a diner but she'd miss it when she left town. Mae was always kind to her and had given her a job even without ID or experience. Charlie, the line cook was a sweet older guy. And Kaylie was a real friend.

Oh God, Kaylie!

With all that was happening with Donnie she'd forgotten all about her friend. At least she'd be in this afternoon so Sally could find out what was going on with her. Maybe she'd made a decision about Devlin and his impromptu proposal.

It would be good to talk to a friend. She kept feeling her eye straying to the clock, waiting for Kaylie to start her shift.

****

"Throw it!"

"Donnie..."

"Come on man! Throw the little bastard."

"Alright..."

Mike the prospect wound up his arm and threw a full beer can. Straight at Donnie's head. Donnie held his fist up and punched the can out of the air, spraying his whole body with beer. He laughed.

"Do another one!"

"Donnie, man I got to get inside and run the bar. It's starting to get busy in there."

Donnie had a moment where he debated pulling rank. Or just beating the shit out of the prospect.

"Okay Whisky Beard. But when I come in, I expect chilled tequila in a glass."

"Chill the tequila? Or the glass?"

"Both man! Jesus."

Mike shook his head and walked inside. Donnie looked around for something else to break. He'd been drinking and breaking things for days now. He was almost starting to enjoy himself.

Almost.

After *she'd* kicked him out he'd come to the clubhouse. That was five days ago. He hadn't been home since. The guys were all giving him a wide berth. Nice Donnie was gone. *Mean* Donnie was in full effect.

So far he hadn't taken any of the sweet butts up on their constant offers to lay or blow him but he was thinking about it. How would Sally like *that?* He frowned. She probably wouldn't care but if she did... well, he didn't want to make her feel bad. He didn't really feel like rolling around with one of those skanks anyway. Not after he'd had her sweet perfection in his arms.

Donnie never lost his head over a woman. He scowled again. Actually he didn't think he'd ever wanted more from a woman than a quick tumble or some head. Oh God... Sally's soft lips would feel incredible on his shaft. He started getting hard at the thought of Sally kneeling in front of him, taking him into her sweet mouth... Christ! He wouldn't let her do that right away though. Not until he'd made *her* explode in *his* mouth.

Hmmm... he just knew she'd taste delicious...

Jesus Christ, he was whipped and he'd never even gotten a taste!

Well, maybe he had gotten a little bit of a taste... of her lips anyway. But that only made him hungrier for her. Even worse though was the fact that she wouldn't let him protect her. She couldn't stop him from driving by her house in his rare moments of near sobriety though. He'd driven by every morning after the bar had closed down around six and again every evening before he got too shit faced. Not that he could tell much with all her curtains drawn.

But maybe, just maybe he'd have a chance to see that she was okay.

Maybe he'd catch that bastard Carl.

He'd been fantasizing about what he would do to that asshole for days. BOOM. He kicked through a piece of scrap wood. That was Carl's femur. SNAP. He took a bat to an old oil barrel. That was the shit heel's head he was busting.

But always the best part, the part that he saved imagining until right before he slipped into the unconsciousness that passed for sleep, was when Sally thanked him. She'd throw herself into his arms. She'd cover him with kisses. She'd lead him to her bedroom where they'd make screechy, rusty music on the old springs until dawn.

And she wouldn't be afraid anymore.

He kicked his boot heel through a piece of plywood that was leaning against the brick wall.

He had to snap out of this. She didn't want him, no matter how she'd responded to his kisses. She'd told him to go away. He wanted to believe that she hadn't meant it. Deep in his gut a little voice said that she didn't really want him to stay away forever.

But maybe she did.

****

Kaylie gave Sally a weary smile as she stowed her backpack under the counter. She looked at her friend and realized that Sally looked worse than she did. Kaylie was at least sleeping a few hours a night. Especially now that she'd decided to talk to Dev again.

She just hadn't told him yet.

"Hey Sally. Busy today?"

Sally shrugged. The girl looked bone tired.

And heartbroken.

"Take a load off, I can handle the tables for a bit."

Sally smiled gratefully and Kaylie got busy, making sure to bring Sally a cup of green tea with lemon.   "Can't drink coffee all day. Unless your stomach is made of iron."

Sally sipped the tea gratefully.

"Thanks Kaylie. My stomach has been a little sour."

Kaylie put her hands on the counter and gave Sally a look.

"So, Janet told me something happened with Donnie."

Sally's eyes got real wide. Guess she didn't realize that bikers gossip too. A lot actually. The clubhouse was like a hive, constantly buzzing about this guy or that old lady. Kaylie hid a smile.

"What did she say? Is he okay?"

"He's been drunk for a week according to Jan. Moping around."

She leaned in and winked.

"Ignoring all the sweet butts."

Sally blinked at her.

"You know what that means right?"

Sally shook her head.

"It means Donnie, who is a legendary ladies' man by the way, is turning down all offers from easy women."

"Oh."

"Sounds like love to me."

Sally shook her head vehemently.

"No. Why would he care? Nothing even happened really. That's the problem."

"That's not what I heard…"

Kaylie picked up the coffee pot and started making the rounds. She knew Sally would be busting a gut by the time she got back to the counter.

"Kaylie! What are you talking about?"

She hid a smile.

"So you do like him. I knew it!"

Sally slumped onto the counter, with her head on her hands.

"I don't want to!"

Kaylie patted her shoulder gently.

"That's always the way. You should have seen Janet! She was cranky as hell until she and Jack stopped dancing around each other."

"Jack dancing?"

"Well, you know what I mean. Now, do you want to hear my news?"

"Oh my God! Yes, please tell me!"

"I'm getting engaged."

Sally stared at her blankly.

"But I thought-"

"As soon as Devlin asks me properly. Talked it over with Mama and we decided it was kind of sweet, him getting ahead of himself that way. Besides, it's not like it's not inevitable."

Sally came around the counter and hugged her quickly.

"That's wonderful Kaylie! Congratulations! Devlin must be ecstatic."

Kaylie winked at her as the dinner crowd started to shuffle in.

"He will be."

"Will?"

"He just doesn't know yet!"

"Kaylie, what?!?"

"Don't worry Sally. I think I have the solution to both of our problems. We are going to out-sweet the sweet butts."

7

Sally opened her door to see Kaylie and Janet standing outside. Janet held a fancy makeup kit and Kaylie had a hanging wardrobe bag over her arm.

"Hi guys. What's all this?"

"Ammunition!"

"We are going out tonight and we are taking no prisoners!"

She stepped aside to let the other girls in. They glanced around at her sparse decor. She knew they saw the bat and the locks but thankfully they didn't say anything.

"I have a shift tonight."

"No you don't. Mae's covering for you with her niece, Becca."

"Oh... why?"

Kaylie and Janet exchanged a glance and smiled conspiratorially.

"Because tonight, we are getting our men back!"

Oh dear.

"You mean get dressed up and-"

"Make their tongues hang out of their heads!"

They laughed but Sally felt sick with nerves at the thought.

"I don't think I can do that Kaylie..."

Janet grabbed her arm and led her into the kitchen.

"Of course you can. I brought everything you need. You're stunning already, we just need to add a little bit of sparkle."

"Oh, I've got plenty of sparkle. I'm just not sure I want to use it."

Janet and Kaylie stared at her expectantly. Sally sighed.

"Come on, I'll show you."

She pulled down the folding staircase to the attic and led them up the narrow flight of stairs. Sally pulled the light cord, bathing the room in stark light. There, in the center of the room, was a huge sparkly pink wardrobe trunk. It stood upright and was covered in the stickers from different venues she'd played over the years. Some pretty big venues too, like BB Kings. She walked over and flipped open the brass locks.

The girls crowded in behind her and she swung the wardrobe open. A rainbow of outfits came spilling out. Most of them were embellished with fringe or rhinestones. Or *both.*

"Oh my God Sally! You weren't kidding!"

Janet pulled out a slinky red dress.

"I bet Donnie would keel over if he saw you in this!"

Sally grabbed the dress and put it back in the trunk.

"Maybe. But he won't ever get the chance to. I'm never wearing any of this stuff again."

She closed the trunk. Janet opened it again.

"Maybe it *is* a little too much for the clubhouse. But I will find you a cute top to wear in here. Trust me."

Kaylie reached into the other side of the trunk and pulled out Sally's favorite performance guitar. It'd been custom designed, with rhinestones covering it from tip to tail. Then she pulled out a CD with Sally's face on it.

"Um, Sally? Is there something you want to tell us?"

She sighed and nodded. She felt something come loose inside her. It felt like such a relief to let go of the burden she'd been carrying for so long.

"Sally isn't my real name..."

****

Three hours later the girls were sitting in the kitchen listening to Sally play her practice guitar. The one without the spangles. Their eyes were wide and weepy as she played them the song she'd written a few weeks ago. The first night that Donnie kissed her.

She finished and rested the guitar on her knee. It felt good to let it sit there. It felt good to play for people again. Even if it was just two instead of two thousand. They were applauding and asking her to play again.

"Just one more Sally!"

"Please? It's so beautiful. I could cry!"

Sally just smiled.

"We better get ready if we are going to this shin dig tonight."

Kaylie and Janet lit up like Christmas trees.

"So you'll go? I wasn't sure after what you told us."

Janet shook her head.

"I'm not surprised you wanted to keep Donnie at arm's length. But he is a good guy. I bet he will surprise you if you let him."

"I know he's a good guy. Why else would he have stuck around with me acting so crazy?"

"You aren't crazy at all and even if you were, you are gorgeous! Lots of guys wouldn't even notice what was going on with you."

Kaylie giggled.

"They'd be too busy staring!"

"Donnie did."

She stood up and put her guitar into it's case. She was going to do it. She was going to go and get him. If he'd have her. She knew it was a risk but she had to try.

"Alright, let's do this. I'm tired of hiding."

The girls whooped and hollered. They each took turns in the shower and dressed, trying on multiple outfits. Except Sally. She only tried on one before the girls stopped her. A pair of tight jeans with a jade green top she used to wear for business meetings. It matched her eyes perfectly. And it didn't have fringe or sparkles on it. It was a bit low cut compared to the stuff she wore now though... They'd giggled at her as she tried to pull it up over her big boobs. Finally she gave up. She never used to feel shy about her body. But knowing she was going to see Donnie tonight was making everything feel ten times more self conscious than going on stage ever had.

She refused to wear a lot of eye makeup though and let Janet focus on dolling Kaylie up. Sally kept her look simple. Her hair was down, parted low on the side and curled just the tiniest bit. Her lips were tinted pink and her applied a thin line of soft brown liner to her upper lids. A dab of cream blush on the apples of her cheeks and she was done.

She stared into the mirror with the girls. They all looked amazing. Heads were going to be turning tonight when they walked in. A blond, a brunette, and a redhead.

They looked like *trouble.*
Sally smiled at her reflection.
She sure hoped so.

8

Donnie pulled on his beer and thought about doing a shot. He wasn't nearly drunk enough yet. Not drunk enough to end this obsession once and for all. Step one was to obliterate himself. Step two was to take the blond girl hanging all over her in the back and take her up on the offer she'd been whispering in his ear all night.

Hell, she'd been making that offer *all week.*

He didn't really care one way or the other. She was alright looking. The only thing he really liked about was that she was a busty blond. Like Sally. But her hair was fake, and her boobs likely were too. Sally had shiny soft hair that always smelled good. And her body... well, suffice it to say that *nobody* had a body like she did. She was a bombshell, plain and simple.

Damn! He couldn't even look at another woman without comparing them to her! They always came up short too. Especially this clingy sweet butt who was starting to annoy him. What was her name again?

Oh right. Melissa. Maybe if he had another shot he'd be inspired to do something with Melissa.

Dev was sitting at the bar again. He'd been there every night this week. They both had. And the girls had been all over both of them, hearing the rumors that they were both single again. This time he had a cheap looking red head trying to get his attention. He ignored her like he always did. He ignored all of them. It didn't stop them from coming though.

All the sudden Dev's head snapped up. The barroom came to a dead standstill. You could literally have heard a pin drop. Donnie straightened up and the blond slid off his arm.

Holy shit.

She was here.

Sally. And Kaylie. And Janet.

But they didn't look like themselves. They looked like themselves, on *steroids.*

His jaw was hanging open as they walked across the bar. He pushed the blond away toward the end of the bar.

"Go on. You can't be back here."

She pouted but he barely noticed. He was too busy staring at *her.*

Sally was wearing tight jeans and a low cut blouse that matched her gorgeous eyes. Her hair was down and styled differently- there was something subtly glamorous about it.

She looked like a God Damn Movie Star.

He felt his stomach turn over. She was the most incredible looking woman he'd ever laid eyes on. And she was staring right at him with a soft smile on her lips. Out of the corner of his eye he saw Devlin sporting a glassy eyed stare at Kaylie who also looked like she'd done something to herself. She looked a lot older than 19, that's for sure.

Jack on the other hand, was growling.

Janet had on a slinky red top that showed off her figure. A little too much for Jack's liking apparently. She waved to him flirtatiously as the girls took up residence at the other end of the bar.

Donnie walked over to them and shoved Whisky Beard out of the way. He barely glanced at Kaylie and Janet. His eyes were on Sally. They were *all over* Sally. And by God, there was a lot to see.

She smiled at him.

He frowned.

"Hi Donnie."

He nodded in greeting, not sure what to say. Was she here to see him? Or drive him insane? What the hell was she up to?

"I'll have a whisky sour please."

"Two mai tais please!"

Janet giggled.

"Kaylie needs her liquid courage tonight!"

He made their drinks quickly. It took an effort to keep his eyes on what he was doing. He had to fight the urge to feast his eyes on her. Devlin waved him over as soon as he delivered their drinks.

"What the hell are they doing down there looking like that?"

Donnie shrugged, his eyes on Sally as she giggled and sipped her drink. She was ignoring him completely. They were all ignoring them. Well, except Janet who kept making eyes at Jack. The two of them were disgusting.

Jack wasn't flirting with his old lady though. He was scowling.

"The whole club is going to be all over them in about thirty seconds."

"Nobody's going to mess with Kaylie."

"Maybe not, but they are going to be all over your girl there Donnie. And ours are going to be right in the middle of it."

"She's not my girl."

"If you ever want her to be, I wouldn't be sitting here talking to us."

Sure enough there were a couple of guys making a beeline for the girls. More than a couple. In less than a minute, there were no less than eight bikers over there, leering at his woman.

His woman dammit.

He straightened up and finished his beer. Then he popped the top off another one and sauntered over there. Sally was laughing at something Dave 'Lugnut' Harris said. Dave was good looking and always had his pick of the sweet butts. Apparently he was looking to branch out. Into *his* territory.

Donnie gave the guy the stink eye until the moron seemed to notice.

"Donnie man, make sure this lovely ladies' drinks are on my tab."

"They're already on the house."

"Oh right, Dev always treats his old lady and her friends. Kaylie you are looking lovely as always. How about another round?"

"Thank you Dave."

Donnie made another round and handed them to the girls. Then he slammed Dave's drink down so that it spilled everywhere.

"What the hell man?"

"*Their* drinks are on the house because I say they are on the house. *Yours* is five bucks. Why don't you go drink that somewhere else Lugnut?"

Dave had the good sense to pay attention. Donnie was always joking around but everyone knew he was dangerous with his fists. He was faster and wilier than anyone in a fight and Dave knew it. Plus he'd been in a vicious mood all week.

"Sorry man. I didn't know she was off limits. Come on guys."

The guys all drifted away under the intense glare that Donnie was giving them.

Kaylie broke the tension with a giggle.

"That was impressive Donnie. Remind me to have you give that look to my economy professor. He's always trying to look down my shirt."

"Who is looking down your shirt?"

Kaylie swiveled on her stool and gave Devlin an arch look. He was looming over her and glaring but she didn't look the least bit concerned.

"Lots of people do. I guess that's because I'm single."

"You're what?"

Devlin looked like steam was about to explode out of his ears. Kaylie titled her head to the side and leaned toward him.

"In the legal sense of the word silly. Everyone around here knows you're my old man."

"Oh I am, am I?"

She nodded and smiled sweetly at him.

"Of course you are."

All the tension leaked out of Devlin's body. He grinned at her stupidly. Then he scooped her up and carried her out of the barroom.

Janet giggled.

"Well, I guess that's that."

Donnie didn't say anything. He was just staring at Sally. He could really see her face with that hair style. She was fucking beautiful. For some reason though, it was making him mad. He poured himself a shot of tequila and threw it back. He caught her looking at him. Something was definitely different tonight. There was a look of warm invitation in her eyes.

Another group of guys were eyeing Sally hungrily. Donnie cursed and jumped over the bar. He grabbed her arm and dragged her behind him to the back and out into the night air.

"Jesus Donnie!"

He let her go and she rubbed her arm. He hadn't meant to be so rough. But she was driving him insane. How much of this was he supposed to take?

To hell with it.

He stepped closer to her and she took a step back. She looked nervous.

Good.

"Do you have any idea what you are doing in there?"

"What are you talking about?"

"You are stirring up all those crazy bastards. You are going to start a God Damn riot in that outfit!"

He took three steps toward her while he ranted. She took three steps back.

"Don't be silly Donnie. It's just a shirt and jeans."

He had backed her up almost to the brick wall. She bumped into it and her eyes widened.

"It's not the shirt. And it's not the jeans."

He braced his hands on either side of her head.

"It's the way you fill them out."

Her eyes were wide as he lowered his head to hers. He didn't kiss her this time, he *took* her. He took everything he'd been wanting all this time. Ever since he first saw her almost a year ago. He took what she'd been holding back. He took it all.

And she let him. In fact, she seemed as wild for him as he was for her. He moaned and deepened the kiss, pulling her soft curves against his raging hard on.

God Almighty but she felt good!

He let his hands do what they wanted to. They seemed to take on a mind of their own, sliding down her back to her high round bottom, grabbing her hips, pulling her tighter against him. He started grinding his hips into hers and she let out a soft whimper. Then her leg was wrapped around his waist and *she* was grinding into *him.*

Fuck. He couldn't take her home. That would require some explanation in advance. Besides it would take too long.

He was going to go insane if he didn't get inside her. Now. Immediately. Fucking *yesterday.*

He couldn't wait. He'd already started unbuttoning her blouse without thinking, his fingers diving into the top of her lacy bra. He had to get her top off. And her pants. Her shoes, she could keep.

He pulled back and stared down at her. They were both breathing hard. One hand was on her chest, and the other one pressed against the wall.

"Take me back to your place."

"Donnie-"

"Damnit woman what are you trying to do to me?"

She just stared at him. He cursed and grabbed her hand, yanking her into the clubhouse and dragging her into the bed room he'd been using all week. It was a mess but he didn't care if it offended her womanly sensibilities. His dick felt like it was going to jump out of his pants and start a God Damn marching parade.

He flung the door shut and locked it. Then he turned to her and smiled. It wasn't a nice smile though. It was the smile of a man who was about to get something he'd wanted for a long time. He took his jacket off and pulled off his shirt. Then he reached for his belt buckle.

"What are you doing Donnie?"

"What do you think I'm doing?"

"Ta- taking your clothes off?"

She looked nervous again. But not afraid. Thank God. He never wanted to make her feel afraid. She didn't say a word, just watched as he kicked off his boots and unbutton the top of his pants, walking towards her.

"Isn't this what you wanted? Isn't this why you came here looking like that? You have to know what you are doing to me."

She shook her head frantically.

"No- I- I mean I did come here to see you. I wanted to talk to you- to tell you I was sorry-"

He stopped undressing. He was less than a foot away than her now. He reached out and brushed her hair away from her face.

"Sorry for what?"

She lifted her eyes to his and they were gleaming with unshed tears.

"Sorry that I pushed you away. You've been nothing but nice to me and-"

"Nice? I'm nice?"

"Yes, and I like you but I was just so surprised that you liked me-"

"Oh so you like me do you?"

She nodded eagerly, clearly hoping he was understanding her.

"And you think I like you?"

Her mouth opened but no words came out. He stared into her eyes.

"I think we can do better than 'like' don't you?"

She blinked at him in that adorable way she always did. Like a sexy little owl. He moaned and lowered his head, kissing her tenderly this time. She *did* like him. She had come here looking like that just to see him. All the anger and frustration flowed out of his body. And was immediately replaced with pure heat.

His tongue tangled with hers as he touched her softly through her clothes, letting his hands wander. That wasn't going to satisfy him for long though. She made no sound of protest when he started unbuttoning her blouse again. She was letting him in at long last. One button, two, three… he moaned as her bra came into view. Her body was fucking glorious. He's never seen a rack like that in his life. His hands cupped her through her bra, stroking her gorgeous tits until her nipples poked up through the lace.

Oh God.

He kissed her again and let his hands slide to her back, reaching for her bra closure. She giggled. She fucking giggled at him.

"What?"

She just smiled and reached for the front of her bra, unclasping it shyly. It fell open and the most beautiful breasts in the world came tumbling out. High and round and oh so voluptuous. He gaped at her, moaning as his hands closed over them.

This right here. This was heaven.

He wanted to taste her but he was too damn tall to get his mouth on her hot little body. He knelt and started worshipping those magnificent breasts, stroking and touching both as he moved his mouth from one to the other.

"Oh Donnie..."

He was making ridiculous slurping sounds as he greedily suckled her. Finally he realized this would be better if her pants were off too. And they were lying down.

He stood up and lifted her off her feet, carrying her to the bed. Gently he laid her down and reached for her waist, placing a kiss on each nipple before he started tugging her jeans down over her hips.

She lay on his messy bed, her blond hair fanned out around her head. She had long perfect legs leading up to an exaggerated hourglass figure. Her hips were sexily rounded and her cute little tummy was flat as a board. And above them... those twin beauties waited. He climbed on top of her and greedily went to work.

****

Sally stared up at Donnie, his beautiful face serious. He intent on lavishing her with kisses. She almost giggled. He seemed to be a little bit, um, focused on her breasts.

Then he lay to the side of her and reached between her legs. Any thought of laughter fled from her mind, along with any other coherent thought. He was stroking her lightly through her panties. He stopped to turn her toward him slightly and lift her leg over his. Then he went back to what he was doing.

Exploring. Tasting. Touching.

And oh God, he knew what he was doing. He knew just went to tease her and when to apply pressure until she was writhing on the bed. But she realized he was doing a lot more teasing than anything else. He bent his leg, lifting hers into the air and spreading her wider. His hand slipped inside her panties at last, sliding up and down her outer lips without trying to push inside.

Her hips were rocking now as Donnie kissed her nipples endlessly and toyed with her femininity. Then he moved his finger to her sweet spot and started a rapid flicking motion.

Oh God!

What he was doing to her defied logic. This huge biker was expertly playing her body like a fiddle! He was keeping her on the brink of orgasm. For almost an hour. In the back room of the Spawns Clubhouse.

And she was letting him. Not just letting him, she was loving it. But she wanted more.

Now.

"Donnie-"

"Not yet."

"Donnie-"

"Not yet."

"Donnie. Take your pants off."

He lifted his head and stared at her, his eyes dark with passion.

"In a minute."

He shifted lower and pulled her panties down part of the way, putting his mouth where his fingers had been. His finger started moving faster but his mouth, oh God, his mouth started kissing her below. He kissed her plump little lips deeply, letting his tongue slip inside her and withdraw with an ever increasing tempo.

Sally was beside herself. She knew she was going to climax soon and it was going to be big. Nothing could stop the tidal wave now except... Oh! He slowed his pace slightly, keeping her release at bay. He lifted his head and blew on her sensitive lips. Now he was just toying with her. Several more times he brought her to the edge and pulled back until she was thrashing on the bed.

Until she was begging.

Finally something changed. He shifted his position and started using his tongue on her clit now. His fingers slipped inside her again and again, opening her up and stroking her slick internal walls. She felt her hips lift up as the world exploded. Her body arched off the bed completely as every muscle in her body tensed and then relaxed. She felt like she was floating back to the bed.

She opened her eyes.

She *was* floating.

Donnie was using his hands to gently lower her back to the bed. And then he was gone. She couldn't see much in the darkened room but she heard the tell tale sound of a zipper.

God bless him. He was taking his pants off.

Finally.

He was on her in an instant, kissing, touching, pressing his hot hard body against her. And boy was he hard. All muscle and silky hot skin. Especially down there. She moaned as she felt his enormous shaft pressing insistently at her belly. He was too big for her... but there was no going back now. Besides she wanted to feel him inside, even if it hurt.

He nudged her thighs apart and guided the tip of his member to her opening, slick with her arousal. They both moaned as he pressed gently forward, edging his way inside her. She felt him stretching her wide, spreading her as he pushed himself inside her. He was barely inside her but he felt so big... no wonder he'd taken so much time to prepare her.

"Sally... oh God..."

He was holding himself back. She could feel the trembling in his shoulders where he was braced above her. He was literally shaking from the effort of not plunging himself inside her again and again.

But that's *exactly* what she wanted him to do.

She let her hands slide down his back to his hips and then she pulled them towards her, urging him deeper inside her. With a moan, he gave in and drove forward, filling her completely. His bare chest pressed into hers and they both gasped at the contact. Then he was kissing her softly as he started to rotate his hips, lazily circling himself in and out of her.

It didn't hurt a bit. It felt… incredible.

Hot and sweet and dirty and *good.*

He kept up the slow and deep rhythm until Sally started to thrash underneath him.

And then he started moving faster.

"Oh!"

She felt herself quickening again. She knew she was getting close. He was too judging from the way his shaft was pulsing inside her. She wanted to make him explode the way he had made her fly up off the bed. She wanted him to lose himself in her...

"I'm sorry- oh God Sally I can't-"

"Don't stop Donnie! Please just-"

He froze above her and then started pistoning in and out of her at a frenzied pace. Her sex felt like it was on fire, her body about to burst into flames. He pumped into her again and again until she cried out and lifted her hips higher and higher. Shockwaves of pleasure tore through her, making her shake as Donnie poured himself into her, his member jerking as his essence filled her up completely.

He didn't stop until the last tremors of pleasure had faded away. Then he kissed her softly and rolled to her side, pulling her with him. He held her without speaking for a long time.

She felt... good. Really, really good.

She hadn't known it could be like this.	The before, the during, *or* the after.

Finally he stirred and started pulling his clothes on. She stood and reached for her bra and panties. She looked up and he was watching her get dressed mournfully.

"I should just keep you in here. Hide your clothes."

She giggled and threw his shirt at him, sighing regretfully as he covered up his gorgeous chest and shoulders. He grinned and held out his hand.

"Come on, let's go."

"Where?"

"Back to the bar."

"But- everyone will know what we just did!"

He smiled at her devilishly.

"I know."

"Donnie!"

She pulled her hand back.

"What? I want everyone to know you are with me."

"You planned this!"

He pulled her in for a kiss but she stood stiffly in his arms.

"No. I didn't."

"Donnie, I'm not going back in there."

"You want to sneak out the back?"

"Maybe I do."

He shook his head.

"No baby. You are with me now and it's time people knew."

He pulled her into the hallway. She went with him willingly enough, though she had her doubts. When they walked into the barroom she was in for an unpleasant surprise.

Kaylie and Devlin were gone. Janet sat at the bar with Jack. She waved them over.

As they walked through the room it erupted in boisterous cheers. The whole place was chanting Donnie's name. Sally's face was red as she pulled her hand out of his grip.

He swiveled his head back toward her.

"I- have to use the ladies room."

He nodded and pointed back the way they had come. She hurried back toward the restrooms as the men slapped Donnie's back. She turned back and saw Janet scolding Jack for giving Donnie a high five. Then she ran.

****

Devlin stared at the woman on his bed. The woman he was trying to make love to.

His woman.

But Kaylie just wanted to talk.

He sighed and paced back and forth in his room above the clubhouse.

Pacing was the only thing keeping him from jumping her.

Maybe if they talked, she'd let him...

"I'm confused Kaylie. I thought you didn't want to get married?"

"No, Dev I said I didn't want to get married *yet*. Besides you never even asked me."

"I asked your mom!"

Kaylie rolled over and pulled her button down shirt shut. He moaned inwardly. Once she started buttoning that thing it would take forever to get her out of it again. He hadn't had her in a week.

And it had been a long week.

He'd spent it wondering if he'd ever get to hold his sweet girl again.

He'd spent wondering if he'd ever recover if he didn't.

"No Devlin. You asked her if she'd like you for a son in law. She said yes. She meant it. She just didn't think you meant right away."

"Is she mad?"

Kaylie shook her head, causing her golden brown waves to ripple over her shoulders. Her clothed shoulders. Well, it was hard to be mad when she was looking so sweetly at him. He could see her white lace bra peeking out from her still unbuttoned shirt.

"No. She thinks it's sweet. And she said it's up to me."

He waited expectantly.

"So?"

She rolled her eyes and reached for her buttons, slipping one into place.

"You are going to have to ask me properly and find out."

He started towards her. Well, if that was all it took-

"With a ring. And not right now."

She sat up and primly started to dress herself. He growled and pounced on her. She squealed as he started devouring her earlobe. He knew that made her crazy. And she smelled so sweet.

He unbuttoned her shirt again, making her laugh and push at his shoulders.

"Devlin! We are having a serious discussion here!"

He lifted his head and stared down as his beautiful girl.

"Yes. We are."

He saw the surrender in her eyes a split second before his lips were on hers, kissing her senseless.

All he had to do was ask.

He'd think about what that meant. But later.

Much later.

9

Sally ran along the dark sidewalks, wiping hot tears off her cheeks. How could he humiliate her like that? He must have known what would happen. Damn him!

She had a moment of regret- imagining how he would feel when he realized she'd run out on him. She knew he wouldn't understand why she was so upset. But she was a private person. She'd learned to protect her personal life when her career had started to take off. What had happened between them was secret and special.

Very, very special.

She'd never felt anything like that in her life. Not even close. He'd shaken her to her core, opened her up with his words and hands and mouth and... then exposed her to the club. It felt like the worst kind of betrayal.

He owed her an apology at the very least. And she owed him- nothing. She'd given him what he wanted already. He'd just have to be satisfied with that.

Besides, she wasn't sure she could go through that again even if she wanted to his girlfriend. Everyone in that clubhouse knew what they'd been doing. They'd cheered for him like she was some sort of conquest.

She felt sick.

Well, she didn't have to go back. She was a free woman. He'd given her one night of unforgettable passion but that was it. They'd both have to move on. She certainly wasn't laying down for him in the clubhouse again. Maybe she should move to another town.

Another state.

The thought of leaving filled her with sadness. She'd made a life for herself here. It was a far cry from the glamorous life she'd had in Nashville, but in a lot of ways it was better. More real. She'd miss it.

She'd miss Donnie most of all.

She walked up to her tiny little house and pulled out her keys. She unlocked the door without thinking.

Without noticing that not all the locks were making that same satisfying thud they usually did.

She walked inside and flipped the light switch.

Something was wrong. Very, very wrong.

"Hello sweetheart."

She spun, reaching out for the bat. It was gone.

Carl was standing in the hallway, holding the bat in his hands.

Sally's whole body turned ice cold. He was going to kill her.

Hell no.

She wasn't going to let him. WHAM

He backhanded her across the face, sending her sprawling into the living room. She scrambled for the couch and the hidden mace under the cushion.

He was laughing behind her.

The bastard was *laughing.*

When Carl laughed like that it wasn't just a bad sign.

It was the *worst* sign.

"Whatcha lookin' for sweetness?"

He walked toward her and she scooted back on her hands and knees as he circled around the room.

"I found all your little toys honey. I've got them now."

He held up her bat, taunting her with it.

"Oh, don't worry. I'm not going to start with this. It would be over too quickly that way. Let's start with an old friend. Then we can warm up to... other things."

He tossed the bat aside and pulled his belt off. She shielded her face as he brought the belt down on her head and shoulders.

THWAP.

Dear God it hurt.

He lifted his arm again and again. Sally stopped trying to figure out a way to fight back and started to pray.

Please lord, save me from this peril. I swear that I will never take the lord's name in vain. I will never-

"Ahhhhhh!"

She couldn't help it. She screamed.

Carl was beating her in earnest, not holding anything back. He stopped for a moment and kicked her with his heavy boots. She peered up at him from between her crossed arms. He was snarling like a rabid mutt.

"Did you lay with him? Tell me, you whore!"

He kicked her again. She was trying to figure out how to get ahold of his foot when he kicked her again, this time in the gut. She rolled over, moaning and clutching her belly.

"Did you fuck him? Tell me!"

He lifted his arm again, raising the belt over his head. She forced herself to answer. Maybe he'd stop if she could convince him.

"Who? I don't know what you are talking about!"

"The guy who keeps riding by! The monkey on the motorcycle!"

Oh God. How long had he been watching her? He must mean Donnie... Donnie must have been riding by unbeknownst to her. Checking up on her. It was sweet of him. It was going to get her killed though. Her silence must have confirmed it for Carl because he threw back his head and stared at the ceiling.

"That's too bad honey. I told you I would kill you if you ever touched another man. But first, I'm gonna kill *him.* Where's he at now? You tell me and I'll make it nice and quick when it's your turn. Otherwise, you and me are gonna have some fun."

Like hell they were!

A sound outside must have distracted Carl because he turned his head for an instant. That was all the time Sally needed. She rolled to her feet and landed a running kick to his gut, knocking him into the entryway. He was scrambling backwards and she rained drop kicks into him until he lay still, with her boot on his throat.

It wasn't exactly textbook martial arts but it had done the trick.

The door crashed open behind her. She didn't turn to see who it was. She didn't have to.

Donnie.

****

Donnie was staring at his tiny little woman. She had her heel on a man's throat. He looked around the place. That must have been one hell of a fight.

The man on the floor was whimpering incoherently.

Good.

He walked over to the sniveling bastard and stepped on his hand until he released the belt he was gripping. He started to roll him over but Sally was frozen in place, obviously afraid to take her foot off his throat.

"Sally, honey let me take over. You did good baby."

He stared at the piece of shit on the floor.

"Real good."

She nodded and pulled her foot back. Donnie rolled the guy onto his face and quickly strapped his arms together. The scumbag had a pistol tucked into the back of his jeans. Donnie used his shirt to pick it up and slide it away from them.

"You got a rope or something?"

She left the room and was back in a minute with another belt. This one was pink. He smiled and tied the bastard's feet. The little shit heel wasn't going anywhere. He pulled out his cell and texted Dev and Jack to bring the guys over and to send a car for Sally. Then he stood up and finally got a good look at her face.

Sally was bleeding. A lot. Her lip, her ear and what looked like a few lacerations around her neck and shoulders.

"Oh honey…"

He took a step toward her but she stepped away from him.

"I'm fine."

"No, you're not honey."

"Don't call me that."

He stopped, confused. She wasn't acting like a damsel in distress who'd just been rescued by her man. Then he remembered. He'd momentarily forgotten that she'd dipped out on him at the clubhouse. He'd forgotten about the ribbing they'd gotten from the rest of the club. Her eyes were narrowed as she stared at him.

Clearly, she had not forgotten.

"Come on now Sally, don't be like that. They were just havin' a little fun at my expense."

"Your expense? What about me? I'm the one who looked like a whore."

He held his hands up.

"No, honey you didn't. They were just happy because I've been mooning over you for so long. They were giving me shit."

She stared at him distrustfully, obviously not sure what to think.

"I swear to you Sally. They were just glad that I wasn't going to be such a bastard anymore. You're my old lady. Or you will be if you can stop being so mad at me. Just say the word."

He held his breath while he watched the emotions play across her beautiful face.

Finally she nodded and dropped her head forward. He pulled her into his arms and held her until the sound of motorcycles could be heard outside.

Dev and Jack walked in first and surveyed the damage.

"Jesus. What the hell happened man?"

Donnie pointed to the tied up man lying on the floor.

"That piece of shit right there."

"We'll take care of him, man. Never to be heard from again."

"No Donnie, you can't! I don't want you to get in trouble."

He stood there, his jaw clenched. He wanted to kill the guy so bad he could taste it. But he wasn't going to do it behind her back. He wasn't going to lie to her.

"You sure Sally? He doesn't deserve to live."

She nodded.

"I know. Just promise you won't kill him Donnie. It's not worth it."

"Alright sweetheart, I won't. There are worse things than death though."

The man on the floor moaned and Jack kicked him. That made Donnie smile.

"Shut up you piece of crap. He did this to you, Sally?"

Sally nodded.

"It's- it's not the first time."

"Oh, but it's sure as shit the last."

Jack cracked his knuckles together and the most terrifying smile came over his face. Donnie knew that he and Dev looked the same.

Carl didn't stand a chance.

Whisky Beard came in and looked around without showing any reaction.

"What do you need?"

Donnie stepped forward, bringing Sally with him under his arm.

"Take her to the ER and then my place. Don't leave until I come back. I'll send a few guys to stand watch at the hospital with you."

"I don't need the ER Donnie. I'm okay... and I don't want anyone looking at me."

He pulled her into his arms and kissed her forehead.

"You sure?"

She nodded.

"Alright, Mike take her to my moms. She'll know what to do. Look at me sweetie."

She lifted her face to him. He felt like crying seeing how brave she was being. He kissed her swollen lips softly, knowing they must hurt.

"You go on now honey. Carl and I are just going to have a little talk."

"Be careful Donnie."

He didn't answer, just waited until she was gone and the car had pulled away from the curb. He pulled out his phone and called his mother.

"Mom. I'm sending someone over. Yeah… it's her. Yes of course I want you to meet her at a sensible hour. It's not like that mom! No- she's been beat up. Yeah. Oh, don't worry. I'll take care of it."

He hung up and looked almost gleefully at the piece of garbage on the floor.

Dev slapped his hand on his shoulder.

"What now brother?"

Donnie picked the bat up off the floor.

"Now shit gets real."

10

Sally was feeling woozy as they pulled up to Donnie's mother's house. It was a beautiful wooded spot just past the edge of town, on what used to be a small farm. Two houses sat next to each other, separated by less than fifty feet. They looked charming, with white picket fences and matching front porches. That's about all she could see in the dark.

"The one next door is Donnie's place."

That explained the two houses.

Mike helped her out of the car and up to the front door. He rang the doorbell.

"Bring her in here son!"

"Yes Mrs. Donahue."

He held Sally around the waist and he guided her to the bright and cheerful kitchen. He eased her into a chair. Mrs. Donahue walked over, wiping her hands on her apron. She was stunning, if older, with long black hair and blue eyes. Just like Donnie's.

"Tsk tsk. Look at you honey. Who did this to you?"

"My ex."

Mrs. Donahue started talking and didn't stop while she gently examined Sally's face.

"Not the first time either was it? Well don't worry, I've got plenty of experience with this. First myself. Then the kids. And then Donnie getting into every scrape he could. I sweat you would think that boy had magnets in his fists."

She pulled at Sally's silk top.

"Take this off honey. You can go now Mike."

"Donnie told me to stick around. Okay if I sit on the porch?"

"Course honey. I'll bring you out some iced tea in a little while. Send Marie in if you see her."

She sat very still while Donnie's mother tended to her. The older woman tsk'd a few more times but was otherwise silent. She knew what she was doing too-being as gentle as possible while thoroughly cleaning all the cuts and abrasions. She finished everything off with an ointment and bandages.

"Best to let some of these breath. Just covered up the worst of them."

"Thank you."

Mrs. Donahue laughed.

"Girl, you're the first woman Donnie's brought home to me. I'd knit you a sweater if you were cold. Now then, you want a bourbon and a lie down? I don't have anything stronger than a Tylenol."

Sally shook her head. She didn't want to fall asleep. Not until she knew that Donnie was okay.

That he hadn't done anything stupid on her behalf.

"No thank you. But I'd like some coffee if you have it."

"Afraid to go to sleep eh? Don't blame you. I don't have coffee though. Just tea."

"That'd be fine, thank you. I just- I just want to see Donnie when he gets back."

That made Mrs. Donahue beam. She brewed a pot of tea and poured Sally a cup. She was sipping it when a beautiful teenage girl came in.

"Come here Marie, say hello to Sally. She's Donnie's good friend."

Marie came over and gave Sally a shy little curtsy. It would have been adorable on a child but Marie was a lovely young woman. She was also simple. That was plain to see when you looked into her eyes.

Sally's heart twisted when she thought about all that this family had been through. She looked around again, not wanting them to see the pity in her eyes. She started noticing the fine craftsmanship of the home. It had been meticulously restored and renovated.

"You have a beautiful house Mrs. Donahue."

"Oh this here is Donnie's place."

"I thought he lived in the house next door?"

"That's Donnie's place too. We live here, but he owns 'em both. The barn too. Though you probably knew that."

Sally shook her head slowly. She had no idea Donnie was so well off. In fact, she had no idea what he even did at all. His mother was looking at her shrewdly.

"You don't have a clue about him do you? Just some pretty boy on a bike with nice eyes?"

Sally frowned. She didn't think of him that way exactly... did she? Mrs. Donahue snorted. Sally had a sinking feeling that Mrs. Donahue didn't think much of her at that moment.

"Here, take this flashlight. Marie, take Miss Sally out to the workshop."

She stood and followed Marie out of the house, hearing Mrs. Donahue muttering.

"How a body could be in love with someone and not know the first thing..."

Mrs. Donahue had a point.

She walked out a well worn path toward a barn about a hundred yards from the house. An enormous willow tree filled the space in front of it. A flat wooden swing hung from one of the sturdy branches above. Marie ran ahead and slid the barn doors open. She flicked a switch and ran back to the tree, hopping onto the swing.

Sally watched her on the swing for a minute. The girl was happy. She knew she was safe and loved.

Thanks to Donnie.

Sally walked into the open barn door and her mouth dropped open. The interior of the barn was modernized, with industrial lamps hanging high above, illuminating the room from corner to corner. There were work tables and heaps of scrap metal everywhere.

But most of all, there was art.

Huge metal sculptures were everywhere. A motorcycle that looked like it could take flight with the enormous wings spread out from the sides. There was an angel that looked like Marie as well as many abstract but beautiful designs. There was another motorcycle across the room that made a shiver run down her spine. It had horns and a tail, almost like a… no it was… a bike fit for the Devil.

How had he managed to make these out of metal? They looked so fluid, like they were molded out of silk. Then she saw the torches lining a high metal rack.

Of course. Donnie was a welder. Well, more than that really. He was a metal smith. And an artist.

An incredibly talented one.

She walked through the barn in awe, with something new to see at every turn.

A small figure hanging from the ceiling caught her eye. It was pirouetting, with long copper hair streaming down it's back. It almost looked alive the way it was spinning on it's wire. She stepped closer to get a better look.

The figure was a woman. Her head was thrown back and there was something wild and free is the way her arms were reaching behind her, almost as if she was about to take flight.

Her heart started pounding in her chest.

It looked like her.

Donnie had sculpted her.

All the fears she'd had about him, all the walls she'd put up, they all came tumbling down in that instant. He did love her. His mama had said so hadn't she?

She stayed in the workshop for almost an hour, touching things and just letting herself revel in her new discovery.

Donnie loved her.

And she loved him.

Finally she went back to the house with Marie following at her heels. Nobody seemed to mind that it was the middle of the night. She showered, wanting to get the slightest hint of Carl's touch off of her. Then she let Mrs. Donahue give her one of Marie's nightgowns and put her to bed like a child.

She closed her eyes and thought about the future for the first time in what felt like forever. She was exhausted. But she didn't sleep. She couldn't. She had to wait for him.

Donnie came home around dawn.

She heard his mother whispering as he came into the house.

"She's resting."

"I just want to see her. Is she going to be alright?"

"She's okay. He got in some pretty bad licks. You said she got in some too?"

"And then some."

"She's quite a girl Donnie."

"I know Ma."

Donnie came into the room she was sleeping it and stood in the doorway. He looked so alone there. She wanted him to come in and hold her.

He stepped forward as she sat up, letting the blanket slide off her shoulder.

"You're awake."

"I wanted to see you."

He came over to her and sat on the edge of the bed. She lay back down and let him stroke her hair.

"He won't bother you again."

"You didn't-"

"Shhhhh... no honey I kept my promise. He's going to have a limp for the rest of his life though."

She held her arms out and he lay down beside her. They stayed like that as the sun came up.

11

Donnie woke up with a start. The bed beside him was empty. He sat up and gripped his hand. He'd jacked it up punching that weasel in the face over and over again, making sure to rearrange some of his features. He wouldn't have such an easy time finding women to terrorize looking like that.

He stretched and went downstairs. His mother was there. Sally was not.

"Where's Sally?"

"She headed out a while ago son. Asked which way was town and off she went."

"What? You just let her leave?"

Donnie knew what she was doing. She was running again. That's what Sally did to protect herself. And now she was running from him. He felt rage and fear welling up inside him.

He wasn't going to let her run away this time. She could try, but he was going to catch her. And he was going to keep her. He ran into his house and grabbed something from his kitchen drawer. Then he was running for his bike.

"Son wait!"

Behind him his mother called out for him but he didn't stop. He couldn't.

Donnie was on his bike in two seconds and blazing down the dirt road at full speed. It was a ten minute ride into town and a thirty minute walk. He made it in five. If he could catch up with her he would make her understand that she belonged with now.

They belonged *together.*

Donnie cruised past her house but she wasn't there. Then he pulled around to the main drag, scanning the streets for her all the way to Mae's.

Nothing.

Damn, where the hell had she gone?

He pulled the bike over when he finally saw her coming out of the fancy new coffee shop that had just opened on the far side of town. She was wearing her tight jeans and one of his old flannel shirts. He felt his stomach settle back into the place it was supposed to be, and out of his throat, where it had been keeping his heart company.

Sally was carrying one of those cardboard take out trays with two large cups in it.

She hadn't run. She was just getting coffee.

The little addict.

He scowled. A man was talking to her. He recognized the guy... It was Jerry, that guy who ran the place where she learned self defense. He'd done a damn good job too. Donnie was about to congratulate him when he saw the way the guy was looking at Sally. She looked annoyed about it too. He was too far to hear what they were saying but he sure as shit saw it when she dumped coffee on the guys lap. Donnie laughed.

"Dammit Jerry, now I have to get more coffee!"

Well, he heard that.

The guy was still there, lurking around when Donnie pulled his bike in front of the coffee shop. He took one look at Donnie and took off. He leaned back on his bike waited for her to come back out.

"You're a caffeine addict you know that?"

She smiled at him and sipped her coffee.

"I got you one too."

He grinned at her.

"I liked the way you disposed of the first one."

She blushed and said nothing, just inhaled more of her precious caffeine.

"Come on, let's go home."

"We better drink it now, it'll spill on the bike."

"I'll get a coffee maker."

She clutched her coffee cup even tighter. He sighed. She was too cute.

"I'll get it today."

* * * * * * * * * *

Sally followed Donnie into the other house, the one he lived in. She looked around curiously. It was just as well kept but a bit messier, and definitely lacked a woman's touch.

"Do you want me to make some eggs?"

He'd convinced her to throw out her coffee and get on the bike with him but she was hungry. Plus she wanted to do something nice for him.

"Not now. I want to show you something."

He locked the front door and pulled something out of his pocket.

Handcuffs.

"That's not funny Donnie."

"I'm not joking."

"But- I have to work later!"

"Not today.

"But Mae-"

"I called her already."

She started backing away from him. Right into the stairwell. She took a step up, trying to reason with him. He did not look like he was in the mood to be reasonable.

"I'm working tomorrow too Donnie."

"I'll let you out for your shift."

He grinned and walked toward her. She took another step up the stairs.

"But then I'm locking you back up again."

She took another step. And another.

"That's good sweetheart. You're heading in the right direction."

He wouldn't really lock her up, would he? She stared into his eyes. His beautiful blue, sparkling, *determined* eyes.

Oh dear. He would.

She turned tail and ran up the steps. He was behind her, lifting her up off her feet and into his arms. He grinned down at her as he carried her to his bedroom. He stripped her clothes off of her methodically and grinned at the outraged expression on her face. Then he slapped the cuff on her wrist and pushed her onto the bed.

Sally stared up at him in awe as he attached the other side of the cuffs to the bed frame. He did it. He actually chained her to the bed!

"You're never going to get away from me now woman."

He was staring down at her triumphantly. But there was something else in his face. Relief.

She realized he'd been afraid of losing her. Her heart swelled at the earnest look on his face. He was half joking of course. He wasn't really going to keep her locked up. Well, maybe for a little while.

She watched him undress that gorgeous body and smiled at him when he joined her on the bed.

"You can lock me up if you want to Donnie. I don't want to be anywhere but here."

He moaned and lowered his body to hers. He was already hard. She spread her legs, inviting him in as he slid into her welcoming sheath. He was breathing heavily already, as if he'd run a marathon. Sally arched her back, bringing them into closer contact, making him groan in ecstasy. He held her face and stared into it.

"You're so beautiful Sally."

She watched him as he made love to her, showing her with his body that what she'd thought last night was true.

Proving it once and for all.

He loved her.

12
Two Years Later

Sally strummed the guitar and prepared to play the wedding march. Well, as well as she could with her swollen belly getting in the way. She liked watching her wedding ring sparkle as her fingers danced over the strings. She looked up and saw Donnie watching her from the rows of chairs.

The church was packed.

Any minute now Kaylie would be walking through that door in a white dress. Funny that Sally had beat her to the alter.

Sally wasn't the only one.

She looked around the church and picked out the large man with wild dark hair holding two squirming toddlers. One adorable little girl with bright red hair was under one enormous arm and an equally adorable little boy with dark hair was tucked under the other. Jack was staring at his wife as she walked down the aisle. Janet was a beautiful bridesmaid. It was a good thing too since none of them had gotten a chance to see Janet in her wedding dress. In fact, no one had known about their wedding until after the fact.

That was mostly just because they had snuck off to Vegas almost two years ago. Less than three months later Janet had been pregnant. Sally loved those kids. Good thing too, since she was their God Mother along with Kaylie. They'd broken with tradition and given the kids two of each. Two God Mothers and two God Fathers.

They really were a family now.

Mae was there, already in tears. In true form she was wearing a bright purple dress and an enormous hat. Her niece Becca sat beside her. She worked regularly at Mae's now that Sally was back to singing full time. Well, she had been before 'the bump' came along.

She smiled when she noticed that Whisky Beard was staring longingly at Becca again. He looked miserable. Just like he always did when he stared at the pretty young girl. Becca was just out of high school and fiercely independent. Sally almost laughed. And so it goes...

The church grew quiet as the doors finally opened. Sally began playing her march as Kaylie drifted down the aisle in a simple white strapless dress that hugged her enviable figure like a glove. The soft white offset her golden coloring to perfection. She looked like a fairytale princess, but not a haughty one. A real one. The wreath of tiny white daisies in her hair completed the picture. Kaylie's mother was the one walking her down the aisle. Mrs. Thomas squeezed her daughters hand and went to sit in the front row.

Tears filled Sally's eyes as Devlin and Kaylie held hands and faced the preacher.

"Do you, Devlin McRae, take this woman to be your lawfully wedded wife? To have and to hold until death do you part?"

Devlin's voice was clear and strong as he answered.

"I do."

"And do you Kaylie Thomas, take this man to be your husband, to have and to hold until death do you part?"

"I do."

"Then by the power vested in me, I now pronounce you man and wife. You may kiss the bride!"

And he did.

We hope you enjoyed Safe In His Arms!

Other Joanna Blake titles include:
Wanted By The Devil (Devil's Riders)
Still Waters (Devil's Riders)
Safe In His Arms (Devil's Riders)
Slay Me (ROCK GODS)

All titles are available at Amazon, iTunes and Barnes & Noble in addition to other retailers.

Sign up for the latest news and special book deals at:

https://tinyletter.com/JoannaBlake

53812996R00283

Made in the USA
Lexington, KY
20 July 2016